JUSTICE DEFERRED

Recent Titles by Jeffrey Ashford from Severn House

THE COST OF INNOCENCE
CRIMINAL INNOCENCE
A DANGEROUS FRIENDSHIP
DEADLY CORRUPTION
EVIDENTIALLY GUILTY
FAIR EXCHANGE IS ROBBERY
AN HONEST BETRAYAL
ILLEGAL GUILT
JIGSAW GUILT
JUSTICE DEFERRED
LOOKING-GLASS JUSTICE
MURDER WILL OUT
A TRUTHFUL INJUSTICE
A WEB OF CIRCUMSTANCES

Writing as Roderic Jeffries

AN AIR OF MURDER
DEFINITELY DECEASED
AN INSTINCTIVE SOLUTION
AN INTRIGUING MURDER
MURDER DELAYED
MURDER MAJORCAN STYLE
MURDER NEEDS IMAGINATION
A QUESTION OF MOTIVE
SEEING IS DECEIVING
A SUNNY DISAPPEARANCE
SUN SEA AND MURDER

JUSTICE DEFERRED

Jeffrey Ashford

severn
House

This first world edition published 2011
in Great Britain and in the USA by
SEVERN HOUSE PUBLISHERS LTD of
9–15 High Street, Sutton, Surrey, England, SM1 1DF.

British Library Cataloguing in Publication Data

Ashford, Jeffrey, 1926-
   Justice deferred.
   1. Painters–Fiction. 2. Art patrons–Fiction. 3. Wife
   abuse–Fiction. 4. Detective and mystery stories.
   I. Title
   823.9'14-dc22

ISBN-13: 978-0-7278-8100-7 (cased)

All Severn House titles are printed on acid-free paper.

Severn House Publishers support The Forest Stewardship Council [FSC],
the leading international forest certification organisation. All our titles that
are printed on Greenpeace-approved FSC-certified paper carry the FSC logo.

Typeset by Palimpsest Book Production Ltd.,
Falkirk, Stirlingshire, Scotland.
Printed and bound in Great Britain by
MPG Books Ltd., Bodmin, Cornwall.

ONE

Mike Linton looked up at Betty, who lay on the bed he'd bought at a jumble sale. It was a cold day, and the gas heater only just kept her warm enough since she was naked. The studio was on the top floor of a small mill, which had been active until some years before it had become unprofitable. Permission to knock down and develop the space had been refused, so the owner had let the bottom floor to a craftsman, who repaired and made antique furniture, and the top floor to Linton. 'Move the left leg a shade closer to the right,' he said.

She did so without comment.

'That's better.' *Safer* was more accurate. His contract would have been cancelled had the magazine had to be shrink-wrapped and placed on top shelves.

It was not work he would have chosen; it was not work to which he willingly admitted. Victorian painters had imbued their paintings with a sexuality which was covert – Etley had offered to introduce a mirror placed strategically for an extra hundred guineas – but his work for the magazine was overt. The editor believed a painting could offer a greater suggestion of availability than a photograph.

He put his brush down. 'OK. Thanks for your help today. I'll just work for ten more minutes or so, and then I can finish without bothering you further.'

'I'm in no hurry, and there's still plenty of the afternoon left, so take as long as you like.'

'I need a break,' he said, and glanced at his watch. Just gone two; it was later than he thought. His stomach rumbled, to underline this. He couldn't remember if he'd eaten breakfast or not – the likelihood was not. Betty was a gem; not many models could lie still for so long without moaning.

Linton reached for the phone with one hand, speed-dialled and placed his order, before picking his brush back up.

He worked steadily for another ten minutes, adding detail to the nearly-finished painting. Betty was a good model. She posed for him because nature had been unkind and granted a beautifully formed body, but inharmonious facial features. Had these matched the perfection of her body, he would never have been able to afford her fees.

There was a shout from street level. 'Pizza, Mike.'

'OK, we'll wrap it up for the day,' Linton said to Betty.

She nodded, then got off the bed, eased her limbs, walked over to the small curtained-area in the corner.

Linton wiped his paintbrush on a rag, dunked it in turpentine. He walked to the door at the head of the stairs. 'Will you bring it up, Ted?' he called.

He crossed to the curtained area and stepped inside. Betty hastily pulled up her minimal lime-green knickers. Like some models, she posed and walked around naked without thought, but was embarrassed to be seen dressing or undressing. 'Sorry, but I need change,' he said quickly.

On the small table against the wall was a cameo glass vase, given to him by an aunt, a great lover of flowers, who had said that whatever he put into it would increase his wealth of pleasure. The money had never multiplied.

Ted, the delivery lad, his long hair tied into a bun which stuck out beneath his motorbike helmet, was looking at the almost complete painting, his juvenile fantasy world turning quickly. 'She's a bit of what-you-fancy! Wouldn't mind your job!'

'I think you'd find it dangerously stressful.'

'Mike,' Betty called out.

Ted jolted, his face flushing. His eyes darted from curtain to painting, his mind making the connection: there, behind the curtain, was the naked object of fantasy that the painting depicted.

Linton tried not to smile. 'Yes, Betty?'

'Have you seen my snakes?'

'Didn't know you'd brought any with you.'

'My brooch, idiot. I took it off and thought I put it in my handbag, but now I can't find it.'

'Sorry, but there aren't any pythons in sight.' Linton turned back to Ted, cleared his throat.

Ted smiled guiltily, remembered why he was there. He took the proffered money from Linton, handed over the boxed pizza, enjoyed a last look at the painting – and a last lingering look at the curtain concealing the goddess – then left.

Betty, dressed in her idea of style, came out of the changing-area. 'I can't find it!'

'Where did you last see it?'

'In my handbag.'

'In which it's now disappeared. Very female!'

She rolled her eyes, then looked at the pizza. 'Are you still eating those things for lunch?' Her tone was accusatory.

'I will be, but this is more a very late breakfast.'

Betty's face took on a look of mild concern. She checked her wristwatch; it dripped diamanté. He wondered if she thought they looked the same as real diamonds, or if she didn't care. 'It's nearly quarter past two!' she said. 'Hardly breakfast. Quarter past two . . . it's hardly even lunch! Why don't you have something which won't clog your arteries?'

'The cooker's in the flat. I'm staying on here to do some honest work.'

'That portrait you're painting? Of that woman?'

Linton nodded. 'A bit of it is causing me grief, and I have to fix it.'

'I want to see it.'

'Not worth the effort.'

'Why do you disparage your own work?'

'Because experience shows my artistic work won't keep an elf alive. I only make money from my nudes.'

'Is it on that easel? I'm going to find out.'

He shrugged his shoulders.

She crossed to an easel which had been turned to face the wall. She dragged it round, revealing a head and shoulders portrait of a dark-haired woman, perhaps in her late twenties or early thirties. She wasn't classically beautiful, but there was a softness to her. She seemed to glow, lit up from something tender inside. After a moment, Betty said: 'Mike, it's really good.'

'I find it difficult to disagree.'

'She's in love with you, isn't she?'

'No.'

'You think one can't tell from the soft, shy smile, the warmth in her eyes? You think anyone can look at her and not know?'

Linton examined the portrait. A muscle in his jaw jumped. 'I hope so.'

'She's married?'

'She hasn't said, I haven't asked,' he lied.

'And you've carefully forgotten to paint her rings? Your ears twitch when you tell a porky.'

'Nonsense.'

'They twitched when you said you needed a break. You want me out of the way because she's turning up.'

'You can believe a dozen unlikely possibilities before breakfast?'

Betty grinned impishly. 'It's well after breakfast, sweetheart. Have fun, and tell her from me she's a lucky woman.' She walked over to where she had put down her handbag. 'When's the next job?'

'No!' Elaine said, her voice shrill.

'Trying to reserve it all for him?' John Cane stumbled as he came forward, awkwardly regained his balance. He was sweating, as he often did when he had been drinking heavily. The clock had barely struck quarter past two when he had staggered in unexpectedly; she'd been touching up her lipstick in the bedroom mirror, getting ready to go to her two thirty appointment.

'He's never tried to touch me!'

'And every slag has a heart of gold. What's his favourite?' he sneered. 'Dining at the Y?'

'Please, John, try to understand. It's never been like you keep trying to think. It only happens in your mind . . .'

'Only in my mind – when I said I'd be back late tonight, but decided to leave early and came home to find you getting ready for your fancy man?' He swallowed quickly. 'And you try to say he only asked you to go there because he wanted to do something to the portrait . . . You think I don't know what he was after?'

'He wanted to correct the left ear. If you hadn't said you'd be late, I'd have told him I couldn't go.'

'And you'd have met me with a loving kiss. Get your clothes off.'

'No.'

'Sodding yes.' He lurched towards her, arms outstretched.

She ran towards the doorway, half-tripped, and he caught her, pulled her round, slapped her face. She hit him. He sneered at her weak blows, but she managed to wriggle out of his grip and reach the passage to the balcony before he caught her a second time and mumbled what they were going to do.

She clawed his face, and the sudden pain caused him to lose his grip. She raced along to the balcony, down the stairs, across to the outside door, opened that, looked back. He remained on the balcony, his balance poor, shouting obscenities.

The Volvo was parked in the garage, which was open. Dreading his reappearance, she climbed into the car, found the keys under the seat, started the engine, backed out quickly. Tears rolled down her cheeks. It was not the first time he had demanded a form of sex she found objectionable; it was the first time he had tried to overcome her resistance by force.

She drove for a while, then parked, staring out at nothing.

After a period of time which she could not judge, and seemingly by chance, she found herself driving back up the incline to her home, Gill Tap. She braked to a halt. To her right, a bulling cow bellowed; a disturbed pheasant flew past, a rainbow of colours almost hidden by beating wings. As happened when he had been drinking heavily, he might have collapsed and passed out. She dithered in the car for a time, unsure what to do. He did not deserve her help, but a sense of responsibility towards her husband, however poorly earned, finally made her decide to return into the house to make certain he had not injured himself or choked.

She walked to the steps down to the front door, hesitated from the brief fear he might be waiting for her because he had correctly judged she would worry about him, would grab her and this time succeed in using his strength to outrage and demean her. She opened the door. Shock kept her silent and motionless until she screamed.

TWO

Constable Tristram Lewis entered the detective sergeant's room. Hopkins looked up, then down at his watch. Bad enough that he was late at the office, without his constable dawdling and dragging things out.

'I had to finish a report for the guv'nor, sarge. He said it was important. A lowly constable has to observe priorities.'

'When I call, I'm priority *numero uno*, Don Tristram.' Hopkins seldom addressed Lewis by his Christian name, because he knew that when he did, there would be resentment as well as sarcasm in his voice. Only someone from the privileged background of Algernon, Hildebrand and Carmichael could be christened Tristram and survive unscathed. If *he'd* been christened Tristram, he'd have had the shit knocked out of him at primary and secondary schools. 'Do you know where Fricton Village is?'

'Used to date a redhead who lived there.'

'In a moated manor house, of course.'

'The moat has long since been filled in, so I suppose it's now a demoted manor house.'

'A stand-up comic! I suppose you now also remember you played spot-the-difference with a blonde who lived in a house called Gill Tap?'

'If I correctly remember the small cottage, the only person who lived there was an old man with a straggly beard who was reputed to eat worms on toast.'

'In a house with a name that daft, I'm almost ready to believe it.'

'"Tap" used to tell people there was a room in the place where one could buy booze, and "gill" meant you'd get a quarter of a pint for the money, only I don't suppose one often did. A smuggling gang once ran the place. The brandy, shipped in barrels from France, was carried from the coast on mules. At the back of the cottage is a slope, so if the excise men were known to be active, the barrels were rolled down into a cultivated jungle of brambles and bracken.'

'You're a mine of unwanted information. The owner of the place has fallen over a banister and landed head first, to the detriment of lasting health.'

'There can't be any banisters there.'

Hopkins felt irritation. 'You know better than the copper who phoned in the report? And being acrobatic, he went up into the air before falling?'

'Can't be the Gill Tap I'm remembering, sarge.'

'You're suggesting there could be two names like that in the county, let alone the same village? Find out what's going on,' Hopkins ordered.

'Why's that necessary?'

'The GP who was called thought the police should have a look,' Hopkins said. Irritation got the better of him. 'If there was anyone else available, I'd send him.'

Lewis went along the corridor to the CID general room. None of the other detective constables was present. He opened the movements book, entered date, time, his name and reason for leaving the station. As he stood upright, he saw on the notice-board, amongst the photographs requesting identifications and memoranda from county HQ, an invitation to all members of CID to a divisional dance. Not for Hopkins, he judged. A dour character, a defender of rules and regulations, tough on mistakes, angered by incompetence, yet always ready to face the annoyance of superiors if one of 'his' DCs was wrongly criticized. Soon after Lewis had joined A division, he had made it obvious he considered that the new detective constable came from a privileged background. He was mistaken. Lewis's father had lost all his capital because his financial adviser had been robbing his clients. Public school had been replaced by state school where, because of his accent and manners, it was only after several fights – in which he had been the victor – that he had been accepted and become one of many.

The remaining CID car was beyond the bays reserved for the brass. Parking in one such had been his first mistake on his first day with the division. He drove out of the car park, waited for a stream of vehicles, drew on to the road. His route took him through streets lined with terraced houses and then past the large building, once an asylum, that was now council offices. There were those who said there had been no need to rename it. He reached the countryside. His family had lived in a sixteenth-century farmhouse until the financial disaster, their extensive land leased to the next-door farmer. As a child, the forty-acre wood had taught him the pleasures to be gained from watching nature. At times, he had sat motionless, resisting the urge to scratch, to blow his nose, to flick aside the stray hair bothering his forehead, as he watched pigeons, jays, magpies, the occasional fox, squirrels, a cock pheasant strutting its stuff and, on one remarkable occasion, a pair of mating badgers. Pleasures now denied to him.

Five miles out from Westhurst, he passed Newton Manor, the home of his former girlfriend – not the mansion Hopkins must have imagined it to be, but, nevertheless, a very well-maintained, ancient house. The redhead had gone to Lady Margaret Hall, Oxford, and had met a fellow student whose father owned a large estate in Norfolk, noted for its shooting. 'Doant thou marry for munny, but goa wheer munny is!' She had liked Tennyson.

Two miles further on, he stopped behind another car outside Gill Tap. He climbed out on to the grass verge and, for a brief, disbelieving moment, thought he had forgotten where to go. The beams in the wall, the steeply pitched, peg-tiled roof patterned with moss, the miniature wrought-iron tun supporting chain and bell, were as he remembered, but rearing up behind the old cottage was an extension which lacked any attempt to meld into the original cottage.

Two steps took him down to the front door. He stepped inside. Under the old roof, there was now open space – a reception hall in estate agents' jargon – and a balcony at the far end. A constable sat on one of the two panel-back armchairs, which were in marked contrast and opposition to other furniture which looked to be Regency. Two oil paintings, in gilded frames, on opposite walls, depicted with Victorian solemnity an elderly man and a woman.

On the floor, beneath the balcony, lay a man. He was partially curled up, one arm outstretched, the other under his body; an uneven semicircle of blood and matter surrounded his head. Lewis swallowed quickly.

'D'you walk here, Trist?' PC Lister asked sarcastically.

'On my hands.' Tristram had become Trist when there was no

longer perverse amusement to be gained from the full name; only Hopkins persisted in calling him Tristram – and, to be fair, only when he was irritated. Tristram wondered why this case had already irritated his sarge, even though it had barely begun.

Lester stood. 'This chair is made of iron. Why don't they have cushions on it?'

'Preserving authenticity.'

'They must have had thick-skinned bums in those days.'

'What's the present situation?'

'The doc is upstairs, calming down the wife.'

'Why's he called us along?'

'Didn't say.'

'Surely he gave some reason?'

'Just advised we should.'

'You didn't think to ask why?'

'I'm just an ordinary copper, so I leave it to you clever ones to ask questions.'

Lewis looked up at the balcony, guarded by a rail and shaped supports, made from a dark, rich wood. He'd have thought them elegant if in a house to which they were suited. 'Have you been upstairs?'

'No.'

'So you've no idea if the woodwork shows any signs of damage?'

'Now there's brains!' Lester had been one of the first to find hilarity in the name Tristram. He played rugger with the divisional team, held the unofficial record for the number of beers drunk after a successful match, considered life was for his enjoyment before that of others.

There was the sound of movement above. A lean man, with sharply featured face, dressed in a suit, carrying a battered case, crossed the balcony and came down the stairs.

Lewis moved forward and introduced himself.

'Dr Waldron . . . Mrs Cane is in bed and sedated.' He looked and sounded tired.

'You asked for someone from CID to come here. Why?'

'Because I had reason to.'

Sharp in features, sharp in character. 'Would you tell me what the reason was?'

'Have you studied the body?' the doctor asked.

'No.'

'Do so now.'

As Lewis neared the dead man, he swallowed hurriedly. Were he to vomit at the sight of violent death, he would again become the butt of jokes in the canteen.

'Look at the neck.' Waldron pointed. There were two deep scratches, almost parallel, on the side of the neck below the left ear. He opened the shirt front. 'Several bruises on the chest, still faintly visible.'

'Were the scratches and bruises caused during the fall?'

'Very unlikely.'

'They are the reason for calling us?'

'Together with other facts. When treating Mrs Cane, I noted a severe bruise on her right cheek; under the nails of two fingers of her right hand was a substance which resembles skin.'

'You think she scratched her husband's neck?'

'I just offer facts.'

'Did you extract what's under her nails?'

'In the circumstances, I would need to seek her permission before doing so.'

'You didn't ask for that?'

'In the excited condition in which she was, any agreement would have been invalid.'

'Would you think it likely there was a fight between husband and wife?'

Waldron did not answer.

'Can you give a time of death?'

'Rigor is progressing, but not advanced – see the tightness of the jaw and neck. Post-mortem lividity is apparent, though of only moderate intensity. These indicators, combined with the temperature of the body, suggest death occurred around three hours before I was called here by Mrs Cane. An estimate that's no more likely to be accurate than usual.'

Making time of death, Lewis quickly calculated, around two to two thirty. He wondered vaguely why a man of middle years should be at home at that time of day, rather than at his office. But given the opulent, if tasteless, surroundings, he was – had been – a man of wealth.

Waldron straightened up and gave the appearance of heading towards the front door.

'Have you been Mr and Mrs Cane's GP for a time?' Lewis quickly asked.

'Since they moved here.'

'Did you know them quite well?'

'"Know" is an ambiguous word. I have met him when he has consulted me with reference to an illness he suffered some time ago. I may have seen her a couple of times, but there has been no social relationship.'

The doctor, Lewis decided, would not have had many social relationships. 'Do you know if there were troubles in the marriage?'

The doctor looked at his watch. 'I must leave.'

'If you could first give an opinion?'

'I do not concern myself with the private matters of my patients.' After a brusque goodbye, Waldron left.

There was a reproduction upright telephone on an oak counter table. Lewis dialled and, as he waited for his call to be answered, wondered if whoever had had the added extension built had ever realized he was guilty of architectural vandalism and destroying evidence of history.

'Yes?' Detective Inspector Bell said.

Lewis quickly made his report.

'You consider it necessary to call out Forensics?'

'Yes, sir.'

'Notified the coroner?'

'I decided to ring you first.'

'Very well.'

Lewis replaced the receiver. He checked the time, was dismayed to find it was getting late, something he would have realized had he noted the approaching dusk. He dialled again, spoke to his future mother-in-law, Mrs Rayner, and asked if he could have a word with Audrey.

'Is something up?' Audrey asked anxiously, over-responding to possible trouble involving him.

'I'm afraid I won't be back for a while.'

'Should I hold your and my suppers back?'

'That would be best.'

He forwent a romantic goodby since Lester was overdoing an attempt to suggest he was not listening. If the delay affected the meal . . . On the way to her home, he would buy a box of truffles at one of the all-night supermarkets.

As the forensic pathologist examined the body, members of the forensic team, dressed in disposable white paper zipper overalls and overshoes, searched the house, calling for photographs to be taken when necessary.

The pathologist stood, picked up his 'murder bag' and crossed to where Detective Inspector Bell was standing. 'Death very obviously caused by severe damage to the skull, the injury consistent with a fall from the balcony. With regards to the time of death, bearing in mind the temperature of the body recorded by the doctor, and other indicators – livor mortis, rigor and so on – I would agree with the previous estimate.'

DI Bell checked his notes. 'Around two to two thirty?'

The pathologist frowned. 'It is an inexact science.'

'But if pressed?' Bell asked, pressing.

The pathologist inclined his head. 'Signs point to the time you mentioned.'

Bell referred to his notes once more. 'And these signs of violence on the body that Dr . . . Dr Waldron noted?'

The pathologist frowned. 'There are five minor bruises on the chest and upper abdomen, probably caused by a fist. Had the assailant been male, I should expect them to have been delivered with greater force.'

'You're saying it was a woman?'

'I am saying that is very possible.'

'But you can't be certain?'

'Without further indications, no. The scratches on the neck may very well have been inflicted by human nails, and I should now like to examine Mrs Cane's hands.'

They made their way upstairs. The large bedroom, in the extension, was tastefully furnished. Elaine Cane lay in the bed, eyes open but face vacant. The female police constable who had been sitting by her side stood up.

'How is she?' Bell asked.

'I think as well as can be expected, sir. She's sedated. The doctor said he'd return later this evening to make certain she was all right.'

'Can she understand what's said to her?'

'I doubt it.'

'Nevertheless, I'll explain things to her in the hopes she can.' Bell approached the bed. 'Mrs Cane, we're very sorry to have to bother you at so tragic a time, but we have to determine the cause of the accident and you may be able to help us. We would like to scrape under your nails. This will cause you no harm. Will you say if you have an objection?'

'Sir, I doubt she—' the policewoman began.

'I note your doubt.'

She argued no further.

The pathologist examined the nails of each hand, used a small wooden spatula to remove any debris under them. The results were placed in two small plastic bottles, each with a label. On these were recorded from which hand the contents had come, and Bell, in spidery letters, wrote date, time, his name and rank.

It was lucky the woman hadn't had the wits to wash her hands, Bell thought morbidly. He spoke to the pathologist, keeping his voice low. 'Is it skin?'

'To the best of my judgement.'

'From the dead man's neck?'

'Tests will confirm that.'

'What about the bruising on her face?'

'Caused by a heavy slap or blow.'

'From the husband?'

'His right hand shows slight signs of contact.'

'Seems there was a heated row.'

'Difficult to think up another possibility.' The pathologist looked at his watch. 'Blast!'

'A problem?'

'Is there ever not? I'm due at an evening meeting of the local residents' association to support an objection to council's actions.' He scratched the back of his neck. 'It's a many layered world, isn't it, when one can examine violent death and then complain about the frequency of collecting dustbins?'

It was not a sequence Bell would have considered. After the other left, he spoke to the SOCO searchers. 'Found anything?'

'This, sir,' one of them, an older man, replied. He picked up a small exhibit bag from the floor. Through the transparent plastic, a gold-coloured, shaped button with a small patch of linen attached was evident. 'Found there.' He pointed to a chalk mark close to the balcony.

'It's been recorded?'

'Of course, sir.' He evidently found the question unnecessary. 'The top rail has been kept well polished, and along where the button was found, there are signs of disturbance, possibly from clothing brushing or scraping it. We have tried to photograph this, but it's not much cop. There'll be a note to the lab to look for traces of polish on the dead man's coat.'

Bell called the policewoman out of the bedroom. 'Go through Mrs Cane's clothes and find out if any has some damage and a missing gold-coloured button.'

She returned into the bedroom, came out with a frock over one arm. 'This was lying on the floor by the bed.' She held it out for him to examine.

Forensics would give their opinion, but he already accepted the button found by the banisters had been torn from this dress.

The duty funeral director, accompanied by two assistants who carried a fibreglass coffin, arrived. The body was lifted on to a polythene sheet, face upwards. After the pathologist had signalled his approval, the sheet was wrapped around the body, secured. Then the wrapped body was placed in the coffin, which was carried out to the van to be taken to the mortuary.

Bell stepped outside and lit a cigarette, in private defiance to his wife who was determined he should give up smoking.

THREE

Lewis and Audrey ate supper in the kitchen since Mr and Mrs Rayner, Audrey's parents, were with friends. Some men might have resented living with the in-laws-to-be, but

Lewis didn't find it too much of a struggle. The savings in rent meant he could save for a ring for Audrey; he could not propose properly until he could afford to buy her one. She had not complained, but he felt the pangs of wounded masculine pride. Living with Mr and Mrs Rayner was merely a temporary setback on the road to domesticated bliss; he had a good woman and he appreciated her. Particularly as she didn't complain when he was late for dinner – again.

'Is something wrong?' Audrey asked, obviously peeved because Lewis had not spoken for a while.

He had speared a piece of beef and a round of carrot, held the fork short of his mouth. 'Why ask?'

'You're looking and acting as if the inspector has given you a right roasting over something.'

'It's just . . .' He stopped.

'Just what?'

'The latest job. The reason I'm back so late tonight.'

'What about it?'

'A man fell from an indoor balcony in his house on to the floor and landed head first. I had to have a word with the doctor, and he insisted I had a close look. I very nearly heaved up.'

She briefly reached across the table and put her hand on his. 'I know what it's like. When I started in surgery and the surgeon began to slice or saw . . . Until I got used to it, I found the best way of distancing myself until I had something to do was to think of Calais.'

'Why there?'

'My first trip abroad with my schoolmates. Eddie's parents had asked him to get some Camembert because it would be tastier than if bought at home. We went into a cheese shop and he asked for some *camelote*. The women screamed at us, called us all sorts of names, one of which I understood. We fled.'

'Was she off her rocker?'

'We reckoned she had to be until I looked up the meaning of *camelote*.'

'Was that Eddie Jones, the little rat who was always trying to persuade you to go to his place to "have fun" when his parents were out?' Lewis asked, feeling jealousy where none was required.

'And never succeeded,' Audrey soothed. 'I've been wondering.'

'How Eddie is?'

'How many children we'll have.'

Lewis put down his fork, beef forgotten. 'What?'

'What's so surprising about that?'

'Well, it's just . . . We're not even officially engaged yet.'

'That's supposed to make a difference?'

'No, but . . .' Talk in the canteen said to delay children until the pressure from the wife became too great. The consequences of becoming a parent were endless. Poverty; broken sleep; demands that the husband get out of bed and rock the child back to sleep or change nappies or mix the milk, despite long days at work; resentment from the wife occasioned by spending a couple of hours enjoying a drink – or two – with one's mates . . .

'You don't want any children?' Audrey said very quietly.

She seemed so distressed that he hurried to persuade her the time could not come soon enough when he held their firstborn in his arms.

Hopkins swore.

'Must you?' Diana asked.

'The bloody fool has missed an open goal.'

She turned over a page of the *Daily Mail*, which she had not had time to read until then.

'They were meant to win hands down, and what happens?'

'From your language, your team is losing. Did you know Timothy Young has died?'

'Never heard of him.'

'He was that famous hairdresser. Celebrities rushed to have their hair done by him. One actress, don't remember which, had him flown out to Monte Carlo before the film festival began.'

'More money than sense.'

'You shouldn't get so bolshy when your team loses. Do you know what he left?'

'A couple of dozen bottles of peroxide.'

'You *are* being difficult tonight. One million, four hundred and twenty-three thousand pounds!'

'I should have forgotten the police and taken up hairdressing.'

She laughed. 'The picture of you telling an old crone how ravishingly beautiful she'll be when you've styled her hair outpaces imagination.'

He used the remote to change channels on the TV. He did not want to see Chelsea go down by double numbers.

'I'd almost forgotten,' Susan said. 'Kathleen has asked us to dinner on Wednesday.'

'I'm unlikely to be able to make it,' Bell replied.

'Why?'

'Work has become a tsunami.'

'I know you find Frank a bit of a pain, but you can make the effort.'

'He's forever complaining the police are becoming too heavy-handed. What would he do in the face of a rioting crowd throwing petrol bombs and rocks? He'd run like hell.'

'He can be a boor, it's true, but Kathleen is charming. Even you have admitted that. She'll be very upset if you don't go.'

'Wednesday is booked twenty-four.'

'How can you possibly know what's happening then?'

'You doubting Thomasine! A job's come in, and that's likely to keep everyone busy for a long time.'

'Has someone robbed a bank?'

'A man fell over an indoor balcony after a fight with his wife. Domestic troubles always cause *us* trouble. So it's better to say no, very sorry, right now, rather than have to ring up and cancel at the last moment and upset all her arrangements as we had to last time.'

'I suppose there is some sense in that, even if you're using it as an excuse . . . How come the man fell over a balcony?'

'The big question mark. But if it turns out his wife helped him over, no one's going to be greatly surprised.'

FOUR

Linton looked out through the window of the small sitting-room in his top floor flat into the darkness. Should he ring again to try to find out how Elaine was? She had been almost hysterical when she had phoned earlier that evening to say what had happened and to demand he tell her what to do. The official-sounding woman who'd answered both of his previous calls to Gill Tap had told him Mrs Cane was unable to answer the phone and, when he had asked why, had said shortly that the doctor's orders were that Mrs Cane was to be perfectly quiet. At least, he supposed, that indicated she'd done as he had suggested and had called her doctor for help. But would the doctor have the time to thoroughly tend to Elaine, when surely he had a . . . a . . . body to deal with?

Poor Elaine. *Poor* Elaine. What a dreadful thing to come home to. He had wondered, when Elaine had not shown up at his studio for her appointment, if her husband had prevented her from coming. And so he had – but in what a manner!

Linton thought he should be feeling happier that the impediment to Elaine's happiness had finally been removed; in the face of her grief and shock, though, he found himself unable to be glad. He would never have wished this on John, if only for Elaine's sake.

He decided to drive out to Gill Tap. He went along the short corridor and down the stairs to the house's back door, which provided him with a separate entrance. As he appeared, his land-lady's Pekinese, rooting around in the garden, yapped, then came over to be patted.

His Volkswagen Beetle was parked several yards along the road. Despite its decrepit appearance, it was serviced regularly and still passed the obligatory roadworthiness tests, as much to his surprise as the inspector's.

He drove out of Westhurst into the countryside, his mind too concerned to enjoy the escape from the suburban sprawl.

Elaine's husband's violent death had, of course, shocked her, but he was worried that although she had lost all love for Cane, circumstances might have had the effect of making her feel falsely guilty. Had Cane not mistakenly believed she was committing adultery, would there have been the accident in which he died? He had abused her, mentally and physically, drunk heavily, given her reason to turn to someone else, but she had never done so. There were still those who honoured honour.

He parked outside Gill Tap, left the car in gear as well as pulling the handbrake hard on, because of the slope. He crossed the grass verge on the concrete path, went down the stone steps to the front door, knocked.

The door was opened by a police constable. 'Yes?'

Surprise was overtaken by fear that there had been further tragedy. 'What's happened?'

'Mr Cane has tragically died.'

'Yes, but how is she? Mrs Cane, I mean.'

The policewoman's eyes narrowed. 'Asleep. It's rather late.'

'I came to find out how she is, but is she . . . is she as well as can be expected in the horrible circumstances?'

'Yes. I'll tell her you called. What is your name?' She flipped open a notebook, ready to write it down.

'Mike.'

'Mike who?'

Linton opened his mouth to reply, then closed it again. Doubt flickered in his mind. Perhaps it would not be wise to give his full name to this sharp-eyed policewoman. Perhaps Elaine would not like it, when she was feeling more herself. 'She'll know.'

'Very well.'

He returned to his car. Before he drove away, he noticed the policewoman had not shut the door and was looking towards him.

He drove to his studio, rather than to his apartment. Once there, he brought out of a makeshift cupboard a three-quarters empty bottle of whisky, poured out a solid tot, added water from the solitary tap over a chipped basin and crossed to the two paintings, now together, so different in form. Betty, crudely nude;

Elaine, dressed with style, but not stylishly. He stared at Elaine, seeing her, not her painting. He had met her at a barbecue party given by Alec, an old acquaintance. Alec, to his silent annoyance, had introduced him to the Canes in jocular style. The van Dyck of the twenty-first century, don't you know!

Cane – pompous, bombastic, red-faced and slightly inebriated, no doubt congratulating himself on being a patron of the arts – had said that for some time he'd been wanting to have a portrait of his wife, and who could paint that better than the modern van Dyck. Ha, ha!

The Italian poet, Padoa, had written love was a problem which only the insane could solve.

By the end of Elaine's first sitting, they were talking freely; by the end of the second, they were comparing likes and dislikes, opinions and judgements; soon, they had accepted they were in love.

He had wanted to take her to bed. She had confessed that she would like to be taken, but she could not bring herself to break her marriage vows, despite her husband's treatment of her. An old-fashioned attitude, which gained his admiration but increased frustration.

He finished the whisky, hesitated before he poured a second, recapped the bottle.

Bell and Lewis walked up the front door of Gill Tap, the overhead light switching on to illuminate the porch as they approached. Lewis rang the doorbell, which made a loud and obnoxious noise.

PC Attwell opened the door, her jaw working in a manner that suggested she was trying not to yawn. She blinked at them both. 'Good morning, sir,' she said politely to Bell and nodded at Lewis.

'Morning. How is she?' Bell asked.

'Still very shaken.'

'Has the doctor been again?'

'Yes.'

'What's the verdict?'

'She's to remain as quiet as possible. He gave her something to keep her slightly under.'

'What are the chances of questioning her?'

The question obviously surprised her. Her jaw hardened.

Perhaps, she thought, Bell had no regard for newly widowed women. He did – but rather less when he suspected them of being the *reason* they were newly widowed. 'I'm afraid the chances are nil,' she said stiffly. 'Mrs Cane is asleep.'

'Damn! I had to come out this way and was hoping to do the two jobs. Have you spoken to her?'

'Only very briefly.'

'Did you learn anything?'

'She didn't mention her husband or what happened.'

Bell made an impatient noise. 'You didn't think to ask one or two questions quietly?'

'Of course not!'

Bell regretted her reticence; the more time between a happening and a witness' statement, the less factual the evidence was likely to be. If Mrs Cane were innocent, it was in her best interests to put her side of the story forward as soon as possible. Delay bred uncertainty. 'Give me a ring when she's fit to be questioned.' He turned to go up the steps to his car.

'Sir.'

'Yes?'

'Yesterday evening, there were two brief phone calls from the same man, wanting to speak to Mrs Cane.'

Bell spoke impatiently. 'You find that remarkable?'

'He sounded very distressed. And not long after, a man drove up and wanted to speak to Mrs Cane. I'm reasonably certain he was the person who phoned earlier.'

Typically, Bell questioned the certainty to test its strength. 'Voices can get distorted over the phone.'

'The line was clear.'

'That's it?'

'When I opened the front door, he was very shocked. Almost panicked.'

'Met by a constable in uniform, I would expect him to be.'

'I told him Mrs Cane's husband had tragically died. He wasn't at all surprised at that, however. He only asked how she was. He seemed very upset about her, almost as if . . . as if . . .'

'Spit it out.'

'As if he was in love with her.'

Female romantic emotion? 'Did you ask his name?'

'Mike.'

'Mike what?'

'He didn't say.'

'You didn't press him to give it?'

'I didn't think I had the right to do so.'

'Unfortunate.'

Her lips tightened.

'Did he come by car?'

'One of those old, original Beetles, pretty well clapped out.'

'I presume you didn't think it worth taking down the number?'

She did not answer.

Bell bit back a sharp comment. 'Colour?'

'Difficult to describe, given the lack of light and the condition of the car, but call it rusty brown.'

'In which direction did he drive off?'

'Facing the road, to the left.'

'Description of the man?'

'Twenty-five to thirty, five feet eleven to six feet, well built, black wavy hair, slightly pear-shaped face, unremarkable features other than an upper lip with quite a peak.'

'Clothing?'

'Casual and haphazard. A very worn green sports jacket with a small tear. Scuffed jeans and beat-up shoes.'

'At least an observer when it comes to clothing.'

Up yours, she thought.

Detective Constable Morgan went down the stone steps to the front door of Gill Tap, entered. PC Attwell, seated on a chair, said sarcastically: 'Do come in.'

'Didn't want to wake Mrs Cane by ringing Big Ben outside. How are things going?'

'Slowly.'

'Nothing to speed time up? No bosom-rippers to read?'

'Does your Aussie mind never climb out of the cellar?'

'Depends how comfortable it is down there. How's the patient?'

'Better, but still confused upstairs.'

'The guv'nor is swearing because you wouldn't let him question her earlier this morning.'

'That man lacks a heart.'

'He wants to know if part-time staff are employed here.'

'And expects me to ask Mrs Cane?'

'Who else?'

'When the doctor said she's to be quiet?'

'Consider Bell's blood pressure. You could keep it down by going up and having a gentle woman-to-woman chat, during which you drop in a question or two, the answers to which will keep the guv'nor in good health.'

'You've no more consideration than he has.'

'You know how things work. The DCS is on the guv'nor's back, so he's on my back, breathing fire.'

'Thought it was half a dozen pints on the way here which had given you a red face.' She stood. 'I'll do my best.'

'I'll give you a kiss as a thank you.'

'I'd rather kiss a frog.'

'Someone already did. Why d'you think I'm here?'

She crossed to the stairs, went up them and on to the master bedroom. He sat – the chair now had a cushion on it – and thought about Bondi Beach with Pamela or Angela, about sun, sea, sand, and grilled fish enjoyed on the shoreline before retiring to his apartment.

She returned. 'There's a part-time daily and gardener two or three afternoons a week. Now you can move out of my chair and leave me in peace.'

He stood. 'Ever been to Sydney?'

'Going there on my honeymoon.'

'You're getting married?'

'How ever did you guess?'

'I come from there.'

'Then we'll think of changing to Melbourne.'

Bell, seated behind his desk, looked up. 'Is PC Attwell still there or has she been relieved?'

'I can't answer, sir,' Lewis replied. 'Morgan didn't say.'

'Find out. If she is, is the daily or the gardener there this morning? If so, go and have a word with one or both; what kind of a man was Cane, and can they suggest someone who knows Mrs Cane and drives an old, worn-out Beetle?'

Lewis left.

Bell began to tap on the desk with the fingers of his right hand, a habit which annoyed his wife. Was PC Attwell correct in her suspicion that the man in the Beetle was emotionally involved with Elaine Cane, or was she romancing? She was a competent officer, which made it reasonable to regard, if not accept, her judgement. In which case . . .

He stopped tapping. There were few original Beetles left on the road, and those that were were usually owned by classic car enthusiasts, yet Attwell had described it as clapped-out and he was prepared to accept that as fact. Members of A division must be ordered to watch out for such a car and to note its number.

Lewis opened the front door of Gill Tap, only to be faced by a woman who wore an apron over blouse and skirt, had a duster in her hand. She stared at him, her round, sharply featured face expressing annoyance. 'Don't you ever knock? What d'you want?'

He introduced himself, apologized for not knocking in the belief there would still be a police constable on duty. 'And you are . . .?'

'Mrs Owen,' the woman replied. 'Part-time daily. That policewoman left earlier, seeing as I would be here.'

'You'd heard about the death of Mr Cane?'

'Not till I got here. I was asked if I'd stay on until Mrs Cane was fit to be on her own, and my dad being gone and Sarah married, I said I would. She hasn't got no family, you see, to look after her. It's a crying shame.'

'I'd like a chat, if you don't mind?'

'Got to get her some grub soon.'

'I won't keep you long.'

He suggested they settled in the sitting room. She hesitated because normally she would not consider doing so, but then agreed.

'How is Mrs Cane?' he asked, once they were seated.

'Poor dear,' Mrs Owen replied. 'I know what it was like when Dad went.'

'Is she still hazy from the dope the doctor's given her?'

'Wouldn't say she's as bright as usual, but there's no wonder to that. She's still in bed; the doctor says she's not to have any visitors under any circumstances.' She shot him a dark look.

'Has she spoken about what happened?' Lewis asked, hoping for something that would please Bell; he knew the news that Mrs Cane was still unavailable for interview would have a poor effect on his superior.

'Not a word.'

'Perhaps one wouldn't expect her to?'

'She likes a chat. Always friendly, always asking how me daughter is. I tell her, getting better slowly after trouble with the second one.'

'Was Mr Cane as friendly?'

'Don't know what he was like before the trouble in his head, but when I first came here, there wasn't nothing friendly about him, and I don't say different just because he's dead. A chicken don't turn into a peacock when its neck's wrung.'

Trouble in the head? Lewis didn't know anything about that; he filed it away for future reference. 'Was he rude as well as unfriendly?'

'When he was, I told him what I thought. Pity she wouldn't do the same. He'd do some work at home, and I'd hear him talk to her like she was a scullery maid. I used to tell her, just because you're a bit younger than him, it don't mean you have to do what he says when he takes that tone. But she wouldn't hear a bad word said against him, told me not to mind him, that it weren't his fault. Silly girl!'

'Did they argue a lot?'

'Takes two to argue, don't it? She just let him shout on.'

'What got him annoyed?'

'Most anything. Why hadn't she been more pleasant to someone they met just because she didn't like the way they behaved; why wasn't she doing this; why was she spending too much on food, a fortune on having her hair done too often. Why, why, why!'

'They were short of money?'

'Not according to what he drank. More than once, I've seen him in the morning with two left feet. I'd of walked out of here but for her. Told her so when I heard him call her a stupid bitch after she dropped something. Said she ought to tell him a gentleman don't speak like that to a lady.'

'Did he ever threaten or strike her?'

'Never known it, but then I wasn't here all that much. And if

I'd seen her with a damaged face, she'd have said it was something else did it, not him. Can't say what he was like before the trouble in his head, but she was too good for him by a mile. Are we done yet? I want to get her some grub, and the house don't clean itself.'

'One last thing. What's the gardener's name?'

'Charlie Woods.'

'When does he work here?'

'Keeps his own times, but he talked about coming the day after tomorrow.'

He stood. 'Thanks for your help.'

She rose too. 'I don't know any more about what happened than you do, it seems, but I'm telling you it'll be a relief for her after she's over the shock.'

PC Clements walked along High Street with the slow, measured tread of a man who had four hours to go before his early turn finished. He stopped in front of a white-goods store and noted the price of a large deep-freeze. His wife said they should have one since it would save money. Politicians used that excuse for their wilder schemes because it was other people's money which would be spent.

He resumed his beat. Passing a charity shop, his attention was caught by the sound of a badly silenced car, and he looked round, saw the back end of an ancient Beetle, brown where there was still paint. He noted the registration number just before the car was hidden from his view, took out his notebook and wrote down time, place and number.

Bell answered the phone and was told that the post-mortem would be held in an hour's time. He asked why he had not been informed earlier.

'You know how things go, Inspector. There's such a rush, it's first things first.'

The call was cut short before Bell had commented on doing first things last. He tapped his fingers on the desk. The results of the post-mortem were predictable, but he needed confirmation they were as predicted.

The phone rang.

'PC Clements, sir. I have just observed an old Volkswagen Beetle, colour brown, in very rough shape.'

'Description of the driver?'

'I only had a very short time to judge, and the car was going away. Around thirty, wavy dark-brown hair, shoddy clothes.'

'The number?'

Clements gave it.

'Keep your eyes open, and if you see it again, check you got the number right.'

'No doubt on that score.'

'After many years in the force, Constable, I've learned two things: check everything, and relieve oneself when there's the chance.'

There was a mildly pained silence. 'I'll remember that, sir.'

Bell replaced the receiver. Another prediction: the DVLA in Swansea would find it would take time to name the owner of the vehicle, and they would have a dozen reasons for that delay. He would be late for the PM if he stayed and used his rank to persuade them to hurry. He used the internal phone to call Hopkins to his office.

Hopkins had barely entered Bell's office, when he learned his fate.

'I have to go to the PM, Bill,' Bell began without preamble.

The use of his Christian name warned Hopkins he might not welcome what he was to be told.

'Constable Clements has rung in to say he's sighted a tattered brown and rusty Beetle and has given the registration number. Get on to the vehicle people in Swansea and tell them we want the name and address of the owner. To avoid the usual bleats about overwork, tell them you're Detective Chief Superintendent Harmsworth and it's top priority.'

'Sir . . .' Hopkins infused the word with as much doubt as he could, without actually having to say that he had doubts.

'The problem?'

'The last time I used his name on your instructions, the person had a query and tried to phone back. Superintendent Harmsworth spent considerable time trying to find out who had used his name illegally.'

'Lightning never strikes twice.'

'There's a man alive who's been struck three or four times,' Hopkins said, but he felt it was a last-ditch attempt.

'A story fit for Ripley's "Believe It or Not".'

Hopkins left, gloomily accepting that no matter what was one's job, those at the bottom of the pile suffered the detritus of those at the top.

FIVE

Bell checked the time, entered his coming trip in the movements' book, left the office. Fifteen minutes later, he parked outside the mortuary. He was not the last to arrive, though a photographer, a forensic scientist and two SOCOs were already there; the pathologist finally turned up, complaining about the roadworks which had held delayed him.

The post-mortem began. The pathologist, as he recorded his actions and findings, examined the crushed head, the scratches on the necks, and the bruises on the chest, now brown and greenish yellow and not readily discernible. He lifted the skin over each bruise to judge whether connective tissues had been crushed. He opened the body and took blood, urine, stomach, liver, and hair samples, which were put into plastic containers and handed to the forensic scientist. The cause of death was certain, but the degree of Cane's drunkenness and the possibility of his having taken drugs had yet to be determined.

The post-mortem completed, the mortuary attendant began to reconstruct the body for viewing by relatives if they so wished. Only God could have reconstructed the head.

The pathologist removed gloves, mask which had covered nose and mouth, white paper zipper overalls and hat. He spoke to Bell. 'The scratches were fairly deep, but the bruises were delivered with little force.'

'With a fist?'

'Probably; not certainly.'

'By a woman's fist?'

'Likely.'

'Could you be more definite? Ambiguities are our worst enemy.'

'You should arrange for more responsive corpses.'

They met irregularly, would not have described the other as a friend, but enjoyed a friendly relationship.

The pathologist put on a sports jacket. 'No signs of internal damage other than from self-indulgence. Do you have reason to expect any cause for the fall other than intoxication?'

'Damned if I know!'

Bell hated uncertainties. He returned to divisional HQ, went up to his room, sat, stared with dislike at the papers on the desk. There was a knock on the closed door. 'Yes,' he called out antagonistically.

Lewis entered. 'I've had a talk with Maggie Owen—'

'It would help if I knew who she was.'

'The part-time daily at Gill Tap, sir. She made it obvious Mr and Mrs Cane didn't get on well. She heard him go on at Mrs Cane for not being pleasant to guests and calling her a stupid bitch because she dropped something. Mrs Cane was quiet and friendly, she says. It sounds as if Mr Cane was an "I-am-somebody" kind of man.'

'Were the rows bitter?'

'Maybe on his part, but not on hers. Seems whatever he said, she put her head down and didn't go at him in return.'

'Did she ever express dislike or hatred?'

'Mrs Owen didn't hear her do so.'

'Her evidence must be taken carefully since it sounds as if she certainly disliked Mr Cane.'

'My guess would be—'

'I dislike guesses.'

'My judgement, sir, would be that she may exaggerate a bit, but it won't be by much. She did add she thought his character had changed for the worse after he had some sort of trouble in his head. That shows she has the sympathy to accept illness can change a man.'

Bell gave glaring at the papers on his desk a rest. 'Trouble in the head? What trouble in the head?'

Lewis remained stoic in the face of provocation. 'If you remember, sir, I mentioned in my report that Dr Waldron – the Cane family's GP – said at the scene that Mr Cane had consulted him several times with regards to an old illness. Perhaps that is what Mrs Owen was referring to.'

'You did not think to enquire?'

'No, sir,' Lewis said.

Bell refrained from comment. 'Is it possible to question Mrs Cane yet?'

'The doctor says no, sir. Mrs Owen was very clear.'

'And you spoke to him personally to confirm this?'

Lewis remained silent.

'Then get on to it immediately.'

Lewis left. Bell made a note: *head trauma*. Could 'trouble in the head' lead to a man falling off a balcony without being helped off it? This case was going round and round in circles; the last thing he needed was further evidence to muddy the waters.

It wasn't long before Lewis returned. 'Sir, Dr Waldron was with a patient, but I spoke to the receptionist, who had been left clear instructions should we call. She said Mrs Cane is too unwell to be questioned; the drugs she is taking would make her evidence unreliable.'

'And her husband's troubled head?'

'The receptionist was not at liberty to say.'

Bell did not feel at liberty to say what was in his mind in response to that. 'Very well.'

Lewis left.

Bell looked down at his papers once more; they failed to enlighten him. He decided to head to the canteen. Black coffee and bacon sandwiches did nothing for the arteries or blood pressure, but they had a certain calming effect on the mind.

Bell left the canteen, went up to his office, closed the door so that someone wanting to speak to him would knock and alert him. He sat. Would Vivien, their daughter, decide to work hard enough to gain entry into Cambridge University or would she be her usual contrary self . . .

The internal phone rang.

'Hopkins, sir. We have the name of the owner of the Beetle. Mr T. Gotski. Lives and works in Arkwright Street – that's to the west of the town.'

'Send someone to find out if he admits knowing Mrs Cane.'

Morgan braked to a halt in front of a name-board set on a brick wall that was topped with broken glass. *T. Gotski and Co. Scrap Merchants.*

He walked through the open gateway and approached a large wooden hut behind a pile of car parts. A fork-lift came round the corner of another heap of household machinery and had to turn as quickly as it could to avoid him. Worth a charge of Dangerous Driving?

He was surprised to find the interior of the hut clean and tidy, intrigued to see seated behind the nearer desk a brunette who reminded him of Sandra – or had she been Joan? – who lived in Rockhampton and whom he would have married had not her verdict of pregnancy been contradicted by a doctor.

'Yes?' Her tone expressed a lack of interest in a handsome, curly-headed, broad shouldered, virile man.

'Is Mr Gotski around?' His Australian accent reminded those to whom he spoke, especially superiors, that an Australian lived a free life in which a detective constable was as good as a chief constable.

'Do you mean Mr Saxecoibanggotski?'

'If that's his stage name.'

'He comes from Bulgaria.'

'I come from God's own country.'

'You need to tell anyone that? What do you want?'

'How about you and me—'

She sharply interrupted him. 'Why do you wish to speak to Mr Gotski?'

'Seeing you, I have the shot and danger of desire for the maid prodigal enough to unmask her beauty to the moon.'

'What are you on about?'

'I'm inspired by Shakespeare.'

'You mean you've heard of him?'

'Lived next to him in Woolanmaroo.'

'You look that worn out.'

The inner door opened and a small, hunched man appeared: head proportionately too large for his scraggy body, unshaven chin midway between smart stubble and sloven forgetfulness, overalls identifying him as a worker amongst dust and dirt. 'You are not here to chat, Miss Robbins.' His accent was strong, but his words intelligible.

'Just being social with a client, Mr Gotski.'

'Social no make money.' He studied Morgan. 'You wish?'

'Thought I'd have a go at selling Sydney Harbour Bridge.'

'Speak to company what thought buying Tower Bridge. You wish business?'

'Detective Constable Morgan.'

'Everything right. No dishonest here.'

'Wouldn't think there could be. I want to talk about the Volkswagen Beetle you own.'

'I do not any more.'

'It's registered to you.'

'I sell.'

'To whom?'

Gotski shrugged his shoulders.

'He may be your best friend, but we need to know.'

'Miss Robbins sell for me.'

Morgan turned to her. 'When was this?'

'Some months ago.'

'You have the buyer's name and address?'

'It was a private sale because the car was Mr Gotski's.'

'You don't know who it was?'

Irritation showed in her face. 'A gentleman saw the "For Sale" notice, came in, asked how much. I told him, and after some bargaining he left and returned with the money. I gave him the keys and papers, and that was that.'

'Tell me about him.'

'Like I said, it was some time back.'

'Was he English?'

'I think so.'

'Tall, short, thin, fat . . .?'

Gotski was making his impatience obvious. He was evidently a man who believed in the aphorism 'time is money'.

'Look, I just don't remember him,' she said, with a nervous glance at her employer.

'My boss will swear when I tell him.'

'You'll be used to that.'

'Shit!' Bell said.

'It's possible she might be able to remember a little more than she told me, sir,' Morgan said.

'Then why the hell didn't you find out?'

'Her boss was around and obviously worried about her talking to me and not working. Bit of a skinflint from the look of him. I reckoned it would be better to question her again when the boss won't be around.'

'Over a pint of Australian gnat's piss you'll try to put down on expenses?'

'The possibility hadn't occurred to me.'

'And one day, you lot will learn to play cricket. Carry on.'

In the CID general room, Morgan crossed to the desk next to his, picked up the telephone receiver on a long lead, returned, sat, dialled.

'Gotski and company,' she said. 'How can I help you?'

'Who's speaking?'

A pause. 'Elizabeth Robbins, Mr Gotski's private secretary. Who am I speaking to?'

'Dis for Mr G. How much he pay for Tower of London?'

'You!'

'Me.'

'What do you want *now*?'

'To see more of you.'

'If you think you're going to unmask my beauty in the light of the moon—'

'Such a thought could only enter the mind of a frustrated poet.'

'Don't waste my time.'

'Do you prefer Italian or Chinese food?'

'English, eaten at home with just my family.'

'Eight thirty tonight at So Hung Low on the High Street.'

'I'm meeting a friend.'

'Ditch him.'

'You don't dislike yourself!'

'Never had cause to.'

'Inspector Bell,' a woman said over the phone, 'Chief Superintendent Harmsworth would like to speak to you. Please hang on.'

As Bell waited, headphones balanced on his shoulder, he stared through the window at the road below. Heavy rain and wind were troubling the umbrellas of unwilling pedestrians. Weather to make a man dream. For the past three or four years, he, Susan and Vivien had holidayed abroad together. Vivien had just declared she was too old to be with her parents and was spending a fortnight next summer with friends in Lesbos. The name of the island stupidly provoked an inference which worried him; as did the contradictory possibility that amongst her intended friends was her newly acquired, shaven-headed, stubbled-chin, cocky boyfriend.

Harmsworth interrupted his gloomy thoughts. 'Bell?'

'Sir?'

'How is the Cane case progressing?'

'The wife hasn't been fit enough to be questioned, and to date we've learned nothing to suggest whether or not she did have a part in her husband's death. Our lead on the Volkswagen Beetle has temporarily dried up, so we don't yet know what part the driver of it might play.'

'You still have not determined whether you're dealing with an accident or manslaughter/murder?'

'I'm afraid not. In addition, the medical evidence contributes to the uncertainty. On the one hand, there is the suggestion that Cane's personality changed for the worse following an illness, which could suggest a motive for murder. On the other, if Cane were as drunk as suggested by his wife, his balance would have suffered. Both provide avenues for enquiry. We will not know further until the PM results come back and until the wife can be interviewed.'

'Keep me informed.'

Bell replaced the receiver. Unlike many senior officers, Harmsworth seldom questioned lack of progress. Unless there was reason not to, the detective chief superintendent accepted that those under his command were conducting a case correctly and efficiently.

SIX

The rain had eased to a drizzle, the wind to a light breeze. Miss Elizabeth Robbins was not waiting outside or inside the restaurant. It seemed she had decided to stand him up, but Morgan was reluctant to acknowledge the possibility and so continued to wait.

Finally about to accept defeat, he started to leave when he saw her begin to cross the road. The street lighting was sufficient to show she had taken trouble over her appearance; despite the bulky mackintosh, she looked smart. As she reached the pavement, he said: 'You look right pongo.'

Her expression showed she wasn't sure whether to smile or slap him. 'What's that mean?'

'I need to teach you about life down under.'

'I don't need to learn.'

He took her arm to lead her into the restaurant; she shrugged his hand away. 'Only trying to be courteous.'

'Thought you said you were Australian.' The tone was sharp, but her expression was soft.

A smiling young woman from Hong Kong showed them to a corner table, handed them menus which offered a plethora of dishes, guaranteed to cause indecisions of choice. He asked Elizabeth what she would like to drink. She chose a dry sherry; he, a scotch on the rocks.

As the waitress cleared the empty dishes, she asked if they would like coffee.

'And a couple of brandies,' Morgan answered.

'Not for me,' Elizabeth contradicted.

'What's the problem?'

'It'll go to my head.'

'After the little wine you've drunk, I guarantee it won't.'

'I wouldn't accept a guarantee from you if it was countersigned by the Lord Chief Justice.'

'The brandy here has very little alcohol in it.'

She laughed. 'You think I'm stupid?'

'No, no! As sharp and attractive a young lady as you'll see in Double Bay.'

'Double talk.'

'Two brandies,' he ordered, grinning.

This time, she failed to refuse.

He guided the conversation until she said: 'Why do you want to know what the man who bought that Beetle looked like?'

'Just interested in what kind of a man buys a car that's coloured rust and brown,' he lied. It wasn't a good lie, but she'd caught him off guard. He was enjoying the evening more than he'd expected. Had, in fact, almost forgotten he was here for a reason.

'How d'you know what colour it was?'

'You said.'

'No, I did not.' She spoke sharply: 'Why did you ask me out?'

'Isn't it obvious? To have the chance of being with—'

'To find out what more I could tell you when Gotski wasn't around, trying to make me work twice as hard as he pays me for.'

It was sort of true, but Morgan felt offended. Couldn't she tell he'd enjoyed the evening? 'You can't really think that!'

'No problem. I must move if I'm to catch the last bus.'

'I'm not going to let a lovely young lady risk her honour by travelling in a public bus at this time of night. I'll drive you home.'

'Putting my honour at far greater risk.'

'I am an honourable man.'

'So was Brutus.'

He drove, to her instructions, to a semi-detached house in South Fricton. He braked to a halt, turned to face her. 'I want to see you again.'

'To find out if I can remember the colour of the man's eyes and hair?'

'I don't give a damn if he has three yellow eyes and green hair. I want to see you because it's you.' He got out of the car, went round the bonnet, opened the passenger door.

'Practising how to be a gentleman?' She stepped out on to the pavement.

'I wouldn't say no to a coffee.'

'My mother always waits up until I return home to make sure I don't entertain undesirable men.'

'She'd find me desirable.'

'She's not gaga.'

'How about another night?'

'You're wasting your time. If I go out, she stays in.'

'I was asking if you'd like to go out for a meal tomorrow evening.'

'No can do.'

'The day after?'

'Sorry.'

'What's the problem?'

'You.'

'Me? I'm harmless.'

'So's a cobra until it bites you.'

'Luigi's, the same time tomorrow?'

'What if I'm not fond of Italian food?'

'Then we'll go to The Ritz and have Russian caviar, Scottish fillet steak and French patisseries.'

'What happens if I say yes?'

'I'll rob a bank before we go up to the Smoke.'

She smiled. 'You're nuts.'

'You're adorable.'

'Goodnight, Brian.' She brought a key out of her handbag, unlocked the door, stepped inside, blew him a kiss before she closed the door.

Sheilas in Rockhampton seldom lived with their mothers, he thought as he climbed back into his car.

Morgan entered Bell's office, walked over to the desk. 'Morning, guv. I saw Elizabeth Robbins last night.'

'Did she provide enough information to identify the driver of the Volkswagen?'

'Things didn't go as smoothly as I'd hoped.'

'Translate.'

'She seemed to think I'd asked her out merely to pump her about the driver.'

'Lacking the art of hypocritical subtlety, your colonial approach was too direct?' Bell asked, with light sarcasm.

'The damage can be repaired. I'm seeing her again, this evening.'

'You don't consider that might have reinforced her suspicions?'

'She'll think I'm after . . . That I like her.'

'If I were she, Morgan, I'd remain suspicious on both counts.'

'You suggested I put down some decent lager on expenses. I didn't think that would get me very far, so I took her out for a meal.'

'With equal lack of success.'

'You did ask me to make contact and find out what I could.'

'So?'

'Shouldn't the meal be an allowable expense?'

Bell drummed on the desk. 'I'm uncertain whether I should subsidize failure. Nevertheless, I'll agree to that.'

'And tonight I've suggested another meal.'

'Don't bother to ask if you can include that as well. To save yourself a heavy bill, tell her you aren't hungry and choose the cheapest item on the menu.'

Morgan turned to leave.

'One moment. Tell Lewis I want him here in half an hour.'

'Gill Tap is a funny name for a house,' Morgan mused.

'You find that funnier than Woolanmaroo for a town?'

'The Aborigines named it.'

'I didn't imagine it was Captain Cook.'

The phone rang. 'Forensics, Inspector. The scrapings from the nails of Mrs Cane are of human skin, very lightly stained with blood. We need to determine the DNA from the blood of the dead man to prove the scrapings came from him. His blood alcohol level was way up the scale of drunkenness. The button is similar in all respects to the other buttons on the dress, and the torn piece of material came from the dress.'

Lewis entered Bell's office, right on time. 'Good morning, sir.'

'It *will* be good if we can make some progress on the Cane case,' Bell said. He looked down irritably at the papers scattered across his desk. The piles had multiplied. So many hard facts and yet not one firm piece of evidence. 'I want you to phone Dr Waldron and get us permission to interview Mrs Cane.'

Bell could see that Lewis was wondering how he could get the aforementioned permission if the doctor did not wish to give it.

'And set us up with an appointment to see the doctor himself,' Bell continued, not giving him space to express such doubts. 'We need some hard facts regarding Mr Cane's medical condition and the changes it wrought in his personality.'

As Lewis left, Bell reflected that since it was looking increasingly likely that Mrs Cane had helped her drunken husband over the edge, it would be quite handy to finally have some evidence to prove it.

An hour later, Mrs Owen opened the front door of Gill Tap.

Bell wished her good morning, introduced himself and Lewis, added, 'We're here to have a chat with Mrs Cane.'

'The doctor won't like that,' she said sharply.

'We've had a word with him, and he confirms it will be all right so long as we don't stay too long.'

'With Mr Cane under the sod, it ain't right.'

'We will be very tactful,' Lewis promised.

'You didn't ought to do it.'

'We would prefer not to, but I'm afraid we have to know what happened.'

'I suppose you'd better come in, then.'

They entered.

'She's in bed, but you ain't going into her bedroom. She was up for a bit yesterday, so maybe she can come downstairs to see you.' She went in to the sitting room, looked around before she allowed them to enter. Bell wondered if she had been making certain all was tidy or whether she was checking what might tempt loose fingers.

Elaine entered the room minutes later, closely followed by Mrs Owen, ready to offer support.

When Elaine was seated, Bell said: 'I'm very sorry to have to worry you at so sad a time, Mrs Cane, but I'm afraid it is necessary. I'll be as brief as possible.'

Her deep-brown eyes were unfocused. There were lines of stress on her face; her hands were gripped together.

'I should like to know how long you had been married.'

It took her time to answer. 'Seven years.'

'You have no children?'

She started to say something, stopped, shook her head.

'Where did your husband work?'

Mrs Owen hostilely answered the question. 'He had his own firm, and if there's nothing more you need to ask, then—'

Bell cut her off. 'What is the name of the firm, and where is it?'

Mrs Owen subsided. 'Choopen Digital Security. It's in Fricton.'

'Thank you.' He turned to Elaine. 'Mrs Cane, was your marriage a happy one?'

'What a dreadful think to ask!' Mrs Owen said angrily.

'It will be quicker for everyone if you don't comment on what I say.'

Mrs Owen silently expressed her opinion of that. Bell wondered if there was a way of ejecting her from the room without trouble; he doubted it.

'Was your marriage a happy one, Mrs Cane?'

Mrs Cane did not reply or acknowledge that he had spoken; she might not have heard.

Bell tried again. 'I imagine, as happens in any marriage, occasionally there were arguments?'

She remained silent.

'Arguments can become rather heated when one of the persons has been drinking heavily.' He waited. 'Medical evidence shows your husband had been drinking very heavily.'

She looked quickly at Bell, then away. Still, she said nothing.

'The doctor who examined you reported you had recently suffered a blow to the face. Had your husband hit you?'

'Yes,' she eventually muttered.

'What was the argument about?'

She shook her head. That the question hugely alarmed her was evident.

'Was it over money?'

'It . . . it's all so confused. I can't remember.'

He judged her to be lying. 'Very well. What happened after he hit you?'

She spoke haltingly, sometimes becoming silent until he thought she would not continue, then doing so. 'I ran to the door, but he stopped me. And . . . and . . . I got free and ran into the passage . . . He caught me, but I managed to reach the balcony and went downstairs, out to the car, drove off . . . ' With eyes closed, she rested her head against the back of the chair.

'We'll not trouble you any more,' he said, before Mrs Owen could order them out of the house.

They drove off.

'They were in the bedroom, had a row, he slapped her hard on the side of the face. What does that suggest to you?' Bell asked.

'That he was a drunken bastard,' Lewis answered.

'Remembering her panic at being asked what the row was about, I'd say there's more to it than just that.'

As they rounded a bend which bordered a village cricket ground, they would have crashed into an ancient Morris in the middle of the road had not Lewis's very quick reactions avoided that.

'Did you get his number?' Bell asked.

'No, sir.'

'Pity . . . What's most likely to have made Mrs Cane as nervous as a cat in a kennel of Alsatians when I asked her what the row was about?'

'Difficult to say.'

'She's worried we might begin to suspect she was having an affair and the husband had discovered this.'

'That can't be right.'

'Your grounds for so definite a judgement?'

'The kind of person she is.'

'If you can judge the true nature of a woman, particularly on so slight an acquaintance, you're way ahead of the rest of us.'

In this one respect, Lewis was convinced he was. His mother had nursed his father through his prolonged, disgusting fatal illness with saintlike care. Elaine Cane did not physically resemble his mother in any respect, yet he saw a similarity in character.

'Did anything interest you about her description of leaving the bedroom after he attacked her, brief though it was?'

'She said she ran out towards the balcony; at the beginning of the passage he caught her again, but she managed to break free. But the button and patch of dress were on the balcony by the banisters, not at the beginning of the passage.'

'Which suggests that that was where they were torn off.'

'The doctor doped her, so probably her memory's fuzzy,' Lewis demurred, annoyed he had found a hole in Mrs Cane's description of events.

'Or hopefully incorrect.'

'She must have been more confused and upset by us.'

'She's convinced you of her innocence? One of the smartest and most charming of women I've ever met fed her husband arsenic for several weeks and tenderly stroked his brow as he died.'

Police work, Lewis thought bitterly, proved that the concept of the essential goodness of mankind was nonsense.

Bell and Lewis approached the receptionist at Doctor Waldron's GP surgery. She did not look up from her typing; instead, she answered the phone when it rang, speaking in a harsh, dismissive tone.

Bell wondered whether he should ding the bell marked 'attention' that lay on the counter in front of him. On reflection, he thought that this would not help matters.

After some time, the woman directed her forbidding gaze at them. 'Yes?' she said, with an air of rudeness.

'Detective Inspector Bell,' he said, showing his ID. 'This is my colleague, Constable Lewis. We have an appointment to see Dr Waldron.'

The woman did not look impressed. 'Take a seat,' she said, waving a hand dismissively.

Bell and Lewis did so; there seemed little alternative.

Bell thumbed through an ancient copy of *Woman's Own*, the cover falling off. In the aisle of seats opposite, a child, accompanied by a harried looking middle-aged woman, coughed incessantly. It was, Bell thought, something like hell.

'The doctor will see you now,' the receptionist barked, indicating a door down a beige corridor.

Bell noticed that even Lewis, eternally polite, did not say thank you.

'I'm not sure how I can help you further,' Dr Waldron began, before Bell and Lewis had barely entered his consulting room. 'I'm a busy man, so—'

'Thank you for seeing us,' Lewis interrupted hastily, evidently sensing that Bell's boiling point was fast approaching. 'We won't take up too much of your time.'

Waldron steepled his fingers. 'Well?'

Bell sat, and Lewis followed his example. 'I am told that you are the GP of the late Mr Cane?'

The doctor inclined his head.

'I understand that Mr Cane had suffered some kind of brain injury . . .?'

'I cannot see how this is relevant to his death,' the doctor said, 'but yes. Some years ago, Mr Cane was unfortunate enough to suffer a ruptured vessel in his brain. He consulted with me several times; I prescribed him medicine to treat the migraine headaches that followed his illness.'

'And that was the only effect of the brain bleed?' Bell asked. 'Did he not suffer changes in personality and temperament?'

'Not being a personal friend of Mr Cane, I find it hard to comment.'

Bell could not help but think that the number of the doctor's personal friends could be counted on one hand.

'But it is common in such cases for the personality to be altered by such a trauma,' the doctor continued. 'Now, if that is all? I have many patients to see.'

'Just one more question. Did Mrs Cane ever see you for any personal injury? Broken bones or similar.'

'Never.'

Bell and Lewis left.

'He wasn't very helpful, was he, sir?' Lewis commented as they drove off.

Bell had nothing constructive to add to that.

Once back at CID, Bell decided to look on the bright side: the doctor's evidence had added nothing helpful, but it had not introduced any further elements of uncertainty. And the interview with Mrs Cane had further suggested her guilt, whilst providing a further avenue for investigation: Mr Cane's business, and the Cane financial affairs.

So far, a potential motive for Mr Cane's murder – if murder it was – remained murky. The romantic affair unproven; the medical evidence inconclusive. But as yet they had not investigated the one motive that lay behind many such 'accidental' deaths: money.

It was a policeman's job to be a cynic, but as he instructed Lewis to look into Cane's business and financial affairs, starting with Choopen Digital Security, Bell admitted to himself that if he found that Mrs Cane was due a large life assurance payout, on top of a large inheritance, he would not be unduly surprised.

SEVEN

As Lewis entered the CID general room, Clements said: 'Just in time to help.'

'Sorry, Vic. The guv'nor wants something done yesterday.'

'Tell him to do it himself.'

'And walk the streets looking for a job? Have you heard of a local business called Choopen Digital Security? Our deceased, Mr Cane, owns it.'

Clements had a slightly lopsided face and rather a long nose. Had he not also had very broad shoulders and strong arms when young, he would have been badly bullied. 'A few months ago, there was a blagging at a firm at the back of Accress Road. Something tells me it was Choopen that installed the security system.'

'D'you know where the company hangs out?'

'In town, but can't say where.'

Lewis went over to the bookcase by the side of the noticeboard, in which reference books and papers were kept when not left out on someone's desk. A description of Westhurst, funded by advertisements, provided the address and telephone number. He dialled, but was disappointed – the number was not in service. That meant he would have to visit in person.

A CID car was available, but he walked since Audrey had

recently expressed her dislike of paunchy men. Choopen Digital Security's offices were on the top floor of a nineteenth century building, once the private home of the first mayor of the town, who had completed his terms of office richer than at the beginning. The outside door was locked, but he heard the sound of movements so knocked.

The door was opened by a man unworried about his appearance. 'You want something?' he asked uninterestedly.

'Who's in charge here?'

'What's it to you?'

'CID.'

'Sorry, mate. I've been checking the electricity. Staff got the push when the company closed up.'

'When was this?'

'Can't rightly say.'

'Any idea what went wrong?'

'Something about being taken to court, so I heard.'

Lewis walked back to divisional HQ.

'What's the picture?' Bell asked.

'I visited Mr Cane's company, Choopen Digital Services, but it seems the company went west for some reason, according to a chap who was doing something to the electricity.'

'Interesting. So perhaps our dead man was no longer as rich as at first appeared. Do we know who Cane's accountants were, and where he banked?'

'Not as far as I know, sir.'

'Get Bill and find out.'

Lewis walked up a gravel path to the front door of a small detached house. He knocked.

Mrs Hopkins opened the door. 'Hullo, Tristram.' Being a Wagner lover, she had neither found the name amusing nor considered the spelling.

'Sorry to disturb you, but did the sarge come back for lunch?'

'He did. Tried to tell me before he left in the morning that he'd eat at the canteen. I said he'd have a solid meal and not something out of a deep-freeze, coated in E-numbers.'

'I need a word with him.'

'Come on in.'

He followed her into the sitting room, which overlooked the small, well-kept back garden. Deep, rhythmic breathing marked the sleeping sergeant, slumped in a chair in front of the television which was switched on.

'Bill,' she called.

He started, did not open his eyes. 'What?'

'Someone's here from the station.'

'Tell him to bugger off.'

'You don't talk like that to the detective inspector.'

He abruptly sat upright. 'I'm sorry, sir . . .' He looked at Lewis. 'Don't you know—'

'I only said it was Inspector Bell to wake you up,' his wife said.

'Real smart!' He looked at his watch. 'I could have had another ten minutes.'

'And still woken up to complain. I'll make some coffee.' She left.

Hopkins ran fingers through his thinning hair. 'What's got you bothering honest people?'

'The guv'nor wants the names of Choopen Digital Security's accountants and Cane's bank. We're to look into it, and sharpish.'

'Why?'

'To find out if he was getting short of cash.'

'Might he have been?'

'We've been told the company's packed it in.'

Hopkins stood, eased his back. 'So what did she gain by helping him over the balcony? Widowhood? Did the mystery driver of the Beetle need to know if her bed was waiting for him? Or did that PC – Jean, or was it Harriet? – get it all wrong about him likely being her lover? Women read too many sloppy romances.'

'We know the car exists, so she can't be making it all up.'

'But her idea of him being all emotionally upset was probably crap.'

His wife entered as he finished speaking. 'Emotional problems always have you scared. Come on through to the kitchen, Tristram.'

After two cups of coffee and three chocolate digestive biscuits, Hopkins had mellowed. 'What do we already know about Cane's finances?'

'Very little,' Lewis answered, 'but you don't live in a house like that and have both a part-time daily and gardener if you need to watch the pennies.'

'But with the firm gone, the wife's likely going to *have* to watch 'em. Unless he's left her a solid life assurance which made him more attractive dead than alive.'

'She couldn't think like that.'

'Trist, wake up to the world you live in. He was a bastard, she has a boyfriend and—'

'Enough!' his wife said. 'This is a no-business-at-home house.'

Lewis drove into the small square area to the side of the house, once a garden, now the occupants' car-park. He and Hopkins left the car, entered the building, walked up to the first floor.

The electrician opened the outside door of the office. 'You're back! What's it this time?'

'We need to have a look around,' Lewis answered.

'I suppose it's all right, and I can give you the keys as I'm just about finished.'

There were four rooms, from none of which had furniture or its contents yet been removed.

'Go through everything,' Hopkins ordered.

'Not much use worrying about most of the stuff, sarge. Anything to do with computers might as well be written in Japanese.'

'If this office is like most, the staff were careless, forgetful or lazy and things got put in the wrong place. We may find what we want.'

'I'd rather bet on the guv'nor giving us a day off.'

Lewis's pessimism was misplaced. Between two pages of circuit diagrams – a spider's trail – was a letter from the company's solicitors which detailed the consequences of the firm's possible liquidation.

The offices of Tamworth and Shuttleleave were in the upper half of Bank Street. The senior partner's office was large, well furnished, had two Baccarat paperweights and framed photographs of wife and daughter on the pedestal desk. Tamworth always listened intently, spoke with much care, and regarded clients' business as information to be guarded at all costs.

'We're making enquiries following the death of Mr Cane,' Hopkins said.

'I understand.'

'We think you may be able to help us, as you acted for his company.'

'Your interest being in the financial circumstances of the company?'

'And his personal ones, if you directly or indirectly acted for him.'

'To deal with the company first.' Tamworth spoke slowly and with a slightly raised voice, indicative of the number of aged clients with whom he dealt. 'It had been charged with negligence, following a large robbery from one of its customers, which resulted in capital and trading losses. When it became clear that one of the company's employees had made a serious mistake in the installation of the system and this was responsible for the success of the robbery, it became inevitable an action would be brought against the company and very likely the court would find against it. Accepting advice, Mr Cane came to an agreement by which he would pay damages and obviate the need and expense of a trial. He had put considerable capital into the business, which would now be lost, as would his income from it.'

'Was he left with enough capital to continue leading a similar life as before?'

'I am not conversant with all of his domestic situation.'

'His wife will inherit what is left?'

'There is nothing left, apart from a small legacy. The house will likely have to be sold to pay the creditors. But she will enjoy the benefit of his life assurance.'

'How much will that be?'

'Seven hundred and fifty thousand pounds.'

'Enough to keep the wolf from the door!'

'The premium was sufficient to cause Mr Cane to query whether he could keep paying it in view of his financial problems.'

'Can you give the name of Mr Cane's bank?'

'He had two separate accounts: one for his private affairs, one for the company's. You would like the bank's name?'

'I would.'

'I will ask my secretary to look through Mr Cane's files and ascertain it.'

'You have authority for obtaining such information?' Gregg, bank manager, authoritarian, nit-picker, enthusiastic kite-flyer asked.

'Since Mr Cane is unfortunately dead and enquiries are being made, that should not be necessary,' Hopkins answered.

Gregg placed his elbows on the desk, raised his arms, joined the tips of his fingers together and stared at the coloured photograph of his prize-winning Sasaki kite. 'You have good reason to require the information?'

Would he have asked for it if he had not? Hopkins contained a belch. Diana was too good a cook for a husband who had been advised to eat less. 'That's right.'

'Mr Cane's private account had an overdraft of well over the agreed limit. We had asked him to reduce it.'

'And he didn't?'

'He was unable to do so.'

'You threatened action?'

'We do not threaten our clients. We informed him of the consequences of his failing to repay the amount.'

'There is a difference?'

'An unnecessary remark, Sergeant.'

'What were the consequences?'

'The usual ones.'

'Then he was in the . . . In a financial hole?'

'A not uncommon occurrence these days.'

Clearly, Gregg had no sympathy, whatever the circumstances, for those who entered into debt.

'Damned hay fever,' Bell said as he put the inhaler down on the desk. 'Can't the pollen give it a rest? It's October, for goodness' sake.'

'They say hay fever comes in the genes,' Hopkins remarked. He eased his position in the chair, which had a rugged seat.

'These days, genes are responsible for every damned thing. If some toerag sticks a knife into your throat because he thinks you looked at him with disrespect, the fault is in his genes, not that he's a right villain.' He sneezed more violently.

'Have you tried antihistamines as well as a spray?' Hopkins asked.

'Every one on the market, and not one does any bloody good.' He dried his nose with a handkerchief. 'What about the bank?'

'Cane was running an overdraft beyond the authorized amount, and the bank was threatening him if he didn't pay it off.'

'Debt to the right of him, debt to the left of him, debt in front of him, engorged and overwhelming.'

'How's that, sir?'

'A man whose company has gone bust, who faces bankruptcy, discovers his wife is probably enjoying another man's bed; *she* finds she's married to a busted flush and recalls that if he were to suffer a little accident then she'd be seven hundred and fifty thou the richer. After giving her hell, he runs into the banisters, becomes unbalanced, and she decides a little push will work wonders for her. In one move, she rids herself of a violent husband, regains her financial security and frees herself to be with her lover. So if we can trace the driver of the Beetle and PC Attwell was right about him, we could be getting somewhere.'

'Looks that way, sir. Not that Lewis will agree.'

'Rose-tinted glasses skew everything.'

EIGHT

Linton sat on his bed, then stood up and paced the room, then sat down again. He should have been at his studio, but he was not one of those artists for whom stress and anxiety encouraged greater artistic effort. When he picked up a brush, his hand shook; not a situation conducive to productivity.

He stood up once more, crossed to his bedside table and slid open the bottom drawer, taking out a bottle of cheap scotch, the seal still intact. Considered it for a moment, then put it back.

Returning to the bed, he sat and put his head in his hands. He could not forget the way the policewoman at Elaine's house had looked at him as he'd left. As if she suspected him of something.

And he had refused to give his last name! He'd thought he'd done that subtly, but perhaps he had been as subtle as a brick.

He broke out in a cold sweat just thinking about it. If the police really possessed such nasty, suspicious minds as those on the television shows he occasionally watched – and from the calculating, thoughtful look on that policewoman's face, he already had his answer – they would automatically think that a man falling from a balcony had not fallen, but had been pushed. And who would they think had pushed him?

They would think *Elaine* had pushed him.

After some time, he sat up straight and squared his shoulders. Elaine had told him what had happened, and the police could not charge her with anything if she was above suspicion. But she would not remain above suspicion if the police discovered that she had a friendship with another man; their nasty minds would immediately leap to conclusions. He made a decision: while every fibre of his being longed to be with Elaine, to take their relationship to the next level now she was freed from her husband, he would have to stay away until the police had stopped sniffing around.

If the police found out that Elaine was in love with another man, and he with her, they would not rest until they had locked Elaine away for the murder of her husband. And he, despite knowing that Elaine was entirely innocent, would be unable to stop them.

Elaine walked the length of the sitting room, stared out through the window at the descending garden which disappeared from her sight when three-quarters of the way down to the bourn.

If only John had not suffered the brain bleed, he might have remained the man she had married. Might not have become an aggressive, unpleasant brute, whom she could never satisfy, no matter what she did. Yet could illness change a man's character so entirely, or did it merely eliminate whatever had been constricting it?

She crossed to the telephone on a piecrust table, picked up the receiver, replaced it, hesitated, picked it up again and dialled.

Linton said: 'I am very sorry, but I am having to work as the alternative to starving, so if you will leave a message . . .'

She slammed down the receiver with hands that shook. She had to speak to him, to gain some release from the blackness which engulfed her . . .

She remembered their private code. She dialled, waited for the third ring, put the receiver down, repeated the sequence.

Her phone rang after a very long minute.

'How's it going, love?' he asked. He sounded strained.

'I've *got* to see you!'

'As I told you—'

'Can't you understand? I have to!'

'We mustn't allow the police to learn about our friendship.'

She felt hysteria rising up. 'Why not?'

'They'll question whether we've been having an affair, my love.'

'We haven't, so they'll know they're wrong.'

'The police aren't conditioned to accept innocence when they see a possibility of guilt. Have they spoken to you yet?'

'Two detectives came along and wanted to know what happened.'

'What did you tell them? As exactly as you can remember.'

Why did he sound so panicked? She clutched the telephone tighter, leant against the wall to steady herself. 'The truth, of course!'

'Did they accept it?'

'They had to.'

'Did they make any comments?'

Why was he asking all these questions? Her head felt cloudy, her legs unsteady. 'What's it matter?'

'Tell me.'

'I can't remember!'

'You must.'

'You're being so beastly! I tell you I can't and you won't listen to me.'

'I have to know so I can help you.'

'Maybe now you'd rather not.'

'I love you, so I need to help you! If you can remember what they said, I may be able to guess what they're thinking.'

Numbness replaced panic. After a moment, she said: 'They asked me if I had had a happy marriage. Said there were always arguments in a marriage, had I had one with John that morning? I told them he was drunk and after a struggle I left the bedroom, that he caught me again at the beginning of the passage and I had to fight my way free.'

'Did they ask you what you meant by "fight"?'

'What's it matter? Stop asking questions. You sound like they did.'

'I'm trying to understand.'

'I've got to be with you. I can't take any more!'

'I've tried to explain—'

'Your work is so much more important than me?'

'You know that's ridiculous.'

'Do I, when you refuse to be with me?'

'If we're seen together and the police find out, they'll wonder who I am, learn I've been painting your portrait and, as I said, come to an absurd conclusion.'

He was being ridiculous, she thought. Why would the police refuse to believe the truth? 'I'll tell them they're totally wrong.'

'Did they ask you why he smacked you so violently on your face?'

'I . . . I think they did.'

'What was your answer?'

'I told them he was so drunk, he had no control over himself.'

'Did they want to know what was the reason for his violence?'

'Mike, I simply can't say. It was all so confusing. I must see you,' she said shrilly. 'I can't carry on if I don't.'

'Meet me on The Last Drop in The Devil's Dyke.'

She almost sobbed with relief.

After replacing the receiver, Linton winced. His distress had overcome his common sense. He had promised himself that he would stay away from Elaine, for her own benefit, and he had already broken that promise. But he assured himself that he had at least chosen somewhere where their meeting could never come to the attention of the police.

Morgan looked at his watch again. Had Elizabeth given him the two fingers and gone off with some witless boyfriend to an upmarket restaurant whose prices she could judge were beyond him? He called her mobile phone; it went straight to voicemail.

Had she switched it off so he could not get in contact with her? He left a short message, trying to sound jovial.

He walked to the Boar's Head and, during the course of drinking three whiskies, persuaded himself he had only asked her out a second time to help add to the case against the Cane woman.

Hopkins, seated behind his desk, looked up as Morgan entered his room. 'What did the woman have to say?'

'She didn't turn up.'

'Then she's a lot smarter than you thought. I'll tell the guv'nor that the lead's died.'

'Before that, I'll give her another bell and find out what went wrong.'

'The gardener at Gill Tap will be there today. Tell Lewis to have a word with him.'

Lewis was in the CID general room.

'Message from the sarge, Trist,' Morgan said. 'Drive out to Fricton, have a pint of real ale at the pub, talk to the gardener at Gill Tap and find out what he can tell us.'

Lewis logged off his computer, left.

Morgan brought his mobile out of his coat pocket, dialled.

'T. Gotski and Company,' Elizabeth said.

'Got any broken dates for sale?'

'I'm so sorry, Brian. The car ran out of petrol because I'd forgotten to check, and when I looked in my handbag for my mobile phone, I found it had run out of battery.'

'Unusual for a woman to make that excuse.'

'By the time I'd got some petrol and reached Luigi's, you'd disappeared.'

'I waited until a smart blonde came up and asked if I was bored.'

'I'm glad I didn't spoil your fun.'

'I drank to my despair.'

'The blonde was unwilling?'

'I told her I wasn't that bored. How about making up for it tonight?'

'I'm babysitting for my sister.'

'I'll come and help you.'

'You haven't been asked to.'

'Only because you thought I might find that embarrassing.'

'I can't think of anything which could do that.'

'What's the address?'

'I think I hate you.'

'Hate is but suppressed admiration.'

'Where did you read that twaddle?'

'The address? I'll bring a takeaway from Luigi's and a bottle of good Aussie plonk to make up for your sorrow.'

Finally, she said: 'Thirty-two Halmers Road.'

As Lewis walked down the steep gravel path, terraced with the land, a stockily built man, on a kneeling pad, weeding with a hand fork, ceased work and stood. Lewis crossed the nine feet between them. 'Keeps one fit, working here with all the up and down.'

'Aye.'

'Detective Constable Lewis. You're Mr Woods?'

'Aye.'

A true son of the soil, Lewis thought. Never miss a weed, never waste a word. 'Very sad about Mr Cane.'

There was no agreement.

'You've been working here quite a time, haven't you?'

'Long enough.'

'There can't be many gardens like this one.'

'Not everyone is bloody daft.'

'I suppose Mr Cane took a great interest in it?'

'Only when he thought I wasn't doing me job.'

'Difficult to know why he should think that when the garden looks as it does now.'

Woods hawked and spat. 'He'll be complaining about heaven if he ain't in hell.'

'Like that, was he?'

Woods became more loquacious. 'Knew Maggie Owen's husband was very poorly, but that didn't stop him shouting at her when she got here late.'

'Presumably, he was a lot more pleasant to his wife.'

'I've heard him talk to her like she was a pikey, not a lady.'

'How did she cope with that?'

'Married to him, wasn't she?'

'Doesn't sound like it was a cheerful marriage.'

'She'd no reason to be happy. If she'd answered him back, it would have been better for her. If he went for me, I told him what I thought. She heard me once. Apologized for what he'd said and explained he'd changed after being so ill.'

'Ever seen or heard him threaten her?'

'If I'd of done, I'd of told him he'd be flat on his back if he laid a finger on her, never mind it'd cost me me job.'

'You weren't here the day he died?'

'No.'

'Had there been any sign of trouble between him and his wife the last time you were here before his death?'

'She wasn't ever going to give him trouble. Too nice for that. Too nice for the likes of him.'

Lewis pointed at a patch of flowers. 'What variety are those?'

'Willow gentian.'

Vivid blue was Audrey's favourite colour. She had recently bought a dress in it which had cost more than she could afford and caused criticism on the grounds of extravagance from her mother. When she wore it, there wasn't an A-list celebrity to match her. 'D'you know where I can get a plant of it?'

'The garden shop on t'other side of town.'

He made his way up the terraced path. All he had learned was confirmation that Cane had been unpleasant. He went round the house to the CID car. However dislikable, he could not believe, as did others, that Elaine Cane had had any part in his death.

The houses in Halmers Road were medium-sized, semi-detached and had cost three times the average wage when built; now they sold for ten times that. Each had a separate garage, bow windows, semicircular fan light with leaded glass above the front door.

Morgan was able to park directly in front of number thirty-two that evening. He picked up the boxed takeaway, the bottle of Jacob's Creek, locked the car, walked through the small garden, rang the front-door bell.

Elizabeth opened the door. 'It's you!'

'Why the surprise?'

'Didn't think you'd bother.'

'You misjudge me.'

'Not by a hair's-breadth.'

As he entered and closed the door, a baby's cries were relayed through a small speaker.

'Upstairs and second bedroom on the right,' she said.

'Now there's a greeting to encourage a man.'

'It sounds as if she wants her nappy changed. You'll find clean ones by the side of the cot.'

'You can't think I'll . . .?'

She laughed as she walked to the stairs.

They finished their meal and went through to the sitting-room. She sat on the settee, he joined her.

'You still haven't asked me about the man in the Beetle,' she said.

He put his arm around her shoulders. 'Never thought of doing so.'

'And I believe in fairies.'

'Plenty of 'em around.'

'You're a homophobic?'

'I'm a live-and-let-live.'

'Steady, junior.' She reached up and lowered his hand. 'Why are you such a liar?'

'My father threw a boomerang, and on its way back it hit me instead of him.'

'Is that why you now suffer from Parkinson's?

'What suggests that?'

'You can't keep your hand still.'

'You know what I really like about you?'

'I know what you'd *like* to like about me.'

'You can stimulate a man.'

'You're asking to be thrown out.'

'I'm talking about brain. You're not like one of those simpering, nineteen-year-old frontispieces in *Country Life*.'

'They'd have you running if they were stupid enough to offer you the chance.'

They heard a car door slam.

'That'll be Daphne and Rob.'

'Your sister and her partner?'

'Husband. Like me, she's conventional.'

'You've too much life in you to be that.'

Elizabeth brushed his arm aside, went into the hall and greeted her sister and brother-in-law, reported their daughter had eaten all her food, been burped, changed and was sleeping soundly. 'Did you have a good evening?'

'Except when Jim had had enough drink to do his quacking duck,' Rob answered. 'Although that's not as bad as his chicken laying an egg.'

'Come and meet Brian. He's a detective. Thought I could help him with a problem and said it was important, so I suggested he had a word with me here. Hope you don't mind?'

'Of course not.'

They entered the sitting-room. 'Hullo, Brian.' Rob shook hands with a firm grip.

Daphne smiled a welcome. 'Have you had something to eat? I'm not certain what was in the larder or fridge, but . . .'

'Brian brought Italian takeaway and a bottle of something he says is wine.'

'A thoughtful policeman.'

'And ambitious.'

Morgan noticed Daphne's quick smile and guessed the intended inference had been understood.

'We'll be moving,' Elizabeth said.

'Must you go so soon?'

'I need a good night's sleep.'

'Some other time, then.'

They said goodbye, drove across town to her home in South Fricton.

He left the engine ticking over. 'You accused me of asking you out tonight because I wanted to question you about the driver of that car.'

'So?'

'Maybe there was something in it the first time we went out.'

'You surprise me!'

'But you don't have to believe in fairies when I say I wanted to see you tonight because of you, not to ask questions.'

'I'm in danger of believing you.'

'Try harder.' He released his seat belt, got out of the car, went round the bonnet and opened her door.

She stepped on to the pavement. 'You've become semi-trained quite quickly.'

'My homage to beauty.'

'A laboured homage.' She crossed the pavement, followed by him, opened the wooden gate, which needed painting, walked up to the front door, brought a key out of her handbag. 'What's the time, Brian?'

'Half ten.'

'I don't know why, I thought it was much later. So, would you like to turn off the engine, come in and have a drink?'

'Won't your mother object? Or might I just pass muster if I don't imitate a kangaroo?'

She went inside, waited for him to enter, closed the door. 'Did I forget to say she and Dad are staying with friends for a long weekend?'

They lay on her bed some hours later. She twisted some of the hairs on his chest.

'Steady on. That hurt,' he complained.

'Thought you were a he-man.'

'Thought I'd proved it.'

She moved to rest her breasts on his chest, kissed him.

'I suppose I'd better get moving,' he said.

'I don't want you to.'

'It may be Saturday tomorrow, but I'm on early turn, and if I don't go now, I'll never make it.'

She lifted off him. He got off the bed, dressed.

'When are your parents returning?'

'Monday.'

'So it's fun again tomorrow night.'

'You don't think it might sound nicer if you were to ask, rather than dictate?'

'You might say no.'

'You couldn't believe you'd be turned down.'

He returned to the bedside. 'You're one perfect sheila.'

'Is that a compliment or an insult?'

'The best compliment an Aussie can offer.' He kissed her, walked over to the door, opened it.

'Brian.'

'Yes?'

'You haven't asked me about the man.'

'Too right.'

'But you were so keen to know if I could tell you anything more about him.'

'If I'd asked you tonight, you'd still believe it was the real reason I'm here. It isn't. I'm here because I wanted to be with you for my own reasons, not anyone else's.'

'You mean that?'

'I'll spit on my toenail to prove it.'

'There are nicer ways. Come and sit by me.'

He settled on the bed, put his arm round her.

'You promise you mean it?'

'How could I lie about that?'

'Without a moment's thought. The man who bought—'

'Forget it.'

'If I tell you now, then when we're next together, I'll know you mean what you say.'

'Even though you think me such a liar?'

'There's really only one more thing about him I can tell you. He could be a painter.'

'Why?'

'There were spots of different coloured paints on the ragged coat he was wearing.'

'A house decorator, or a do-it-yourself nut?'

'I can't believe even the modern decorators would use one or two of the colours on him. I reckon he may be an artist. No reasonable person would dress so carelessly unless he has to live on baked beans; nor would he buy such a wreck of a car.'

'Some artists make a fortune.'

'This one doesn't. And stop doing that or you'll never get to work.'

NINE

Morgan walked into the detective sergeant's room. 'Morning, sarge.'

Hopkins studied him. 'Been on a bender for the past twenty-four hours?'

'Couldn't sleep.'

'Try a small mug of warm milk before going to bed.'

'Doubt that would've worked. My mind was busy.'

'That makes a change.'

'Last night, I used my manly charms to talk to Elizabeth Robbins.'

'Did you learn anything?'

'The man who bought the car may be a painter: a starving artist, not a house painter.'

'Why does she think that?'

'He was dressed in someone's cast-off clothes and had splodges of different coloured paints on them.'

'Doesn't sound right.'

'Why not?'

'Mrs Cane wouldn't associate with someone like that, surely. She keeps herself as neat as they come, even now.'

'Can't think that has much to do with it.'

'If you'd ever had the chance to meet a woman who's classy, you'd know Mrs Cane wouldn't spend time with a tramp.'

'Choice depends on the inner soul, not the outer cover.'

'Training to wear a dog collar? Still, I suppose we ought to follow up the idea since it might help keep the guv'nor below boiling point.'

'I read in the local rag that there are one or two artists who live in the area. Seems the light is right for them.'

'You're mixing up Westhurst with Polperro.'

'I know there's one shop which sells paints and brushes, so there must be someone around who wants them.'

The phone rang. Hopkins had a brief conversation, replaced the receiver. 'Find out their names.'

Hopkins picked up a sheet of paper which listed the duty shifts for the coming week, left his office and went into Bell's.

'Get me Lewis in half an hour's time, would you?' Bell asked. 'I think we'll have another crack at Mrs Cane.'

'Of course.' He handed the list across the desk. 'Morgan's managed to have another word with the Robbins woman, sir.'

'And?'

'She thinks the driver of the car is an artist.'

'For what reason?'

'Badly dressed, and there were splatters of different coloured paints over his clothes.'

'An imaginative deduction.'

'It's all we have. And it seems there are a few artists around. There's at least one stationer in town which stocks paints, brushes and whatever else they use. I've asked Morgan to dig out some names.'

'How did he persuade the Robbins woman to speak up?'

'Seemed better not to ask.'

Green and Co, stationers, dated back to the end of the nineteenth century. Judging by the lines on Abbot's face, remaining wisps of hair carefully placed, heavy jowls and stooped back, he could have started not all that long from the time it opened.

He caressed his chin with forefinger and thumb. 'Yes, there are some artists around, but not enough to make stocking their materials profitable. We do that as a convenience for them.'

'Can you give me names?'

'Let me think . . . There's Mr Hicton-Smith, who works in the summer at sea resorts, painting holidaymakers; does quite well in a good summer, but always tries to get a discount from us. Never does. There's Lin something . . . Linton. Specializes in page-three-style nudes, with little extras added. Can't think of anyone else . . . That's wrong. Romax. There are a couple of others who come occasionally, but I've never had reason to know their names.'

'Does one of them drive a beat-up Volkswagen Beetle?'

'Won't be Mr Romax. Likely, his is a Rolls or a Bentley.'

'What about any others?'

'Can't suggest what they could be driving if they don't have to make-do with bicycles. That is, except for Mr Linton. Not long back he was complaining about the cost of having a car repaired for the fourth time, so he likely has one.'

'What kind of a man is he?'

'Friendly, usually cheerful, watches the pennies. Talks like he comes from better than he is.'

Bell stood back from the front door of Gill Tap as Lewis rang the bell. As usual, it made him wince; money did not buy taste. Such a loud, obnoxious chime was only one notch classier than a bell that played a tune.

There was no answer for some time. Then, suddenly, the door shot open, revealing the form of Mrs Owen, clad in a frilly apron and rubber gloves.

Blast, thought Bell. He'd hoped that he could interview Mrs Cane without her resident watchdog.

'What do you want?' Mrs Owen said rudely. 'You upset her, last time you was here. I hope you're not here to upset her again?'

Bell did not have the patience for this. Luckily, he had a constable who knew the routine.

'We'll try our best not to upset Mrs Cane,' Lewis said diplomatically. 'We just need to have another quick chat with her, clear up a few things. Is she awake?'

Mrs Owen gave him a hard stare. 'She is. I suppose you'd better come in.'

She ushered them into the sitting room once more and left them twiddling their thumbs for some time.

Finally, Mrs Cane entered, with Mrs Owen – sans rubber gloves and apron – following close behind.

No cup of tea offered, once again, Bell noted.

Mrs Cane looked better than she had last time – still pale and distracted, but her eyes were less vacant. She sat, and her fingers worked together anxiously.

'Mrs Cane, I hope you are feeling a bit better?' Bell asked, feeling sympathy.

'Course she ain't feeling better!' Mrs Owen interjected angrily. 'With her husband so newly passed!'

Mrs Cane put up a wavering hand, and Mrs Owen subsided. 'I feel . . . a little more myself, thank you,' she murmured.

Her eyes darted back and forth, Bell noticed. Last time, they had been dull and unseeing; now, she seemed unwilling to look him in the eye. He wondered if that had significance.

'We are sorry to trouble you again, but we have a few further questions,' Bell said.

Mrs Cane looked alarmed. Her fingers tightened together so hard they went pale. She said nothing.

Bell spotted his chance. 'Perhaps Mrs Cane might benefit from a soothing cup of tea?' he said.

Mrs Owen shot him a suspicious look, but bustled off.

'Mrs Cane, tell us how your husband was before his brain injury,' Bell said.

Mrs Cane's lips drooped. 'He was as I'd hoped, exactly,' she said, very quietly. 'Polite, warm, friendly. Didn't change once we were married, either – anything I wanted for the house, he bought it for me. Anything he could do to help, he did it.' Tears welled up in her eyes.

Bell, alarmed, looked around for a box of tissues, but Mrs Cane had rescued a handkerchief from her cardigan pocket and was dabbing at her eyes.

'And how did he change after his accident?' Bell asked.

Mrs Cane sat, seemingly lost in thought, for a moment.

'Mrs Cane? After the accident?'

She seemed to stiffen. She straightened her spine and her lips firmed. 'It wasn't his fault,' she said. 'It was the ruptured blood vessel. He nearly died, you see.'

'Was he violent?' Bell asked baldly.

Mrs Cane hesitated. 'No, not . . . I mean, he was never what I'd call violent. Just bad tempered. He must have been in pain a lot; he had headaches,' she said. 'He didn't mean to be as rude as he was!' she said, sounding rather desperate now. 'He . . . he . . . he . . .' She subsided miserably. 'I couldn't do anything right. But I married him, for better for worse!' she added defiantly. 'It wasn't his fault that he changed. It was the illness that made him the way he was!'

Mrs Owen bustled back in, carrying a tray. She put it down and glared at Bell and Lewis. 'What have you been asking her?' she snapped.

Bell noted that the tray contained tea for one – Mrs Cane. 'Merely trying to get a fuller picture,' he said. He turned back to Mrs Cane. 'Would you describe your marriage as a happy one after your husband's unfortunate change of personality?'

'I . . . I . . .' Elaine stammered. Her hands gripped the handkerchief and colour rushed to her face.

'You've got a right nerve, asking a grieving widow such a thing!' Mrs Owen snapped. 'I said it when you asked that before, and I'll say it again – it's a dreadful thing to ask!'

'It's a simple question,' Bell said mildly. 'Mrs Cane?'

'I . . . It was happy once,' Mrs Cane said, tears flooding to her eyes. 'It w–w–was happy once!' Tears flowed down her cheeks, and Mrs Owen put an arm around her.

Murmuring apologies, Bell rose, indicating to Lewis that he should do the same, and they left the house.

'It's looking more and more certain that we can get her for manslaughter, at the least,' Bell mused as they drove off.

'I don't see why, sir,' Lewis said.

'I'm just thinking out loud, here, Lewis. Picture the scene: a drunken husband punches his wife. She tries to defend herself, but he grabs her. She escapes down the hall, and he pulls at her clothing, ripping it. They grapple on the balcony; he loses his balance, and she – fearing for her safety – gives him a little push over the edge. The real question is whether she helped him over out of self defence, or because she wanted to be rid of an obstacle to her happy future.'

'I still don't think she had anything to do with it, sir,' Lewis said.

'You don't, eh? Still think she's whiter than white?'

'She just doesn't seem the type, sir.'

'Well, Clements is following up on the artist who owns the Beetle, so we'll soon see if PC Attwell's romantic suspicions are confirmed. If the good woman was having an affair, it'll be all the evidence we need to bring her in.'

'D'you watch the telly a lot?' Linton asked as he modified the curve of Betty's right breast.

'When I get the chance,' she answered. 'Trouble is, Dad and Mum only like soaps.'

'You don't?'

'You're surprised?'

'It was a straight question, free of any inference. What's your choice?'

'Ballet, orchestras.'

He stepped back, studied the painting. Betty now had tight curly black hair, an elongated face, dark-brown eyes, lips which offered much, a slightly exaggerated body in an exciting pose. He was satisfied her appearance differed from any in the past six paintings. The art editor wanted a different model in each issue of the magazine, but since he refused to increase the fee, Linton altered Betty. Simple, but crude, changes, like natural pubic hair, rather than Betty's habitually trimmed and shaped bush, made a significant difference; Linton suspected, gloomily, that the men who viewed his paintings rarely spent much time looking at his model's face, in any case.

DC Clements walked through the doorway.

'What the devil do you think you're doing?' Linton demanded. 'Never learned to knock and be invited in?'

Clements looked away from Betty, with obvious difficulty. 'Sorry. Thing is, the road door was open and there was no bell, so I came on up. Detective Constable Clements.'

Linton felt a sudden unease; tried to conceal it.

'Mike, you're about to be arrested for obscene paintings,' Betty said laughingly. She walked over to the 'changing room' and went inside.

Clements said, dragging his gaze away from the curtain that concealed Betty: 'I'd like a chat with you, Mr Linton.'

'About what?'

'Your car.'

Linton began to clean his brushes, using the time to try to still fears.

'You have one?'

'Yes.'

'What make is it?'

'Volkswagen.'

'What model?'

'A Beetle.'

'Colour?'

'Brown.'

'A new, modified one, or an original classic, restored and looking sharp?'

'Original and unrestored.'

'Have you been in Fricton recently?' There seemed to be an increased interest in the policeman's tone of voice.

'Could have been.'

'On Tuesday?'

'It's possible.'

'At what time?'

'Can't really say.'

'Perhaps in the mid evening?'

Linton shrugged his shoulders.

'Did you call at Gill Tap to ask how Mrs Cane was?'

Panic overwhelmed him; he kept his face on his brushes in an attempt to quell it. 'Who?'

'Mrs Elaine Cane.'

'I'm supposed to know her?'

'Do you deny that?'

'I neither deny nor confirm. And if you would be kind enough to leave, I can get on with my work.'

'Mr Cane had unfortunately suffered a fatal fall, and Mrs Cane understandably was in a state of shock. A police constable was in the house to offer what support she could, and a man called and was very concerned about Mrs Cane. I think that man was you.'

Denial momentarily seemed the only option. 'It wasn't.'

'PC Attwell can be called to identify you.'

After a pause, Linton muttered: 'Yes.'

'It was you?'

'Yes.'

Betty, dressed, walked across to Linton. 'Be seeing you, Mike.' She briefly waited for him to explain the presence of the detective. When he didn't, she left.

'How did you know Mr Cane had suffered a fall?' Clements asked.

'I didn't.'

'Then why were you so concerned about her well-being?'

'She has not been well recently,' Linton invented, 'and the last time she was here, I thought she looked ill.' He wished he had thought up a convincing story beforehand, wondered how on earth the policeman had tracked him down.

'Why does she visit you?'

At least a portion of the truth could be revealed without danger. 'Because of her portrait.'

'You are *painting* her?'

'I did not make that clear?'

'I like to have facts confirmed so that they cannot later be denied.'

'I have for some time been painting her, at the request of her husband.'

'You are friendly with her?'

'I try to be. Build up a rapport with the sitter and she relaxes.'

'Your rapport is perhaps a strong one.'

'If that is a statement, you're not in a position to make it. If a question, the answer is: I am no friendlier with her than I am with any sitter.'

'Do you always ask after them if you have reason to think they're not well?'

'It's a courtesy I like to make.'

'D'you think other painters are as thoughtful?'

'I cannot answer what others do or don't do.'

'Are you sometimes in Mrs Cane's company when she is not being painted?'

'No.'

'PC Attwell was of the opinion you were probably emotionally involved with Mrs Cane.'

'Women seek emotion.'

'She is trained to judge unemotionally.'

'Whatever emotion she thought she observed was a mistake for sordid commercial worry. Had Mrs Cane been very ill, there had to be the possibility she would not recover for a long time and my fee would be delayed.'

'Thank you for your help,' Clements said, sounding as if he did not mean his words. 'I may be seeing you again.'

Linton tried to regain the upper hand. 'Please announce your

arrival before you enter so that you don't embarrass my sitter
again.'

'I have to say, she did not look very embarrassed.'

Clements left, satisfied Linton was worried far more than his
manner had shown.

Linton uncapped his 'emergency' bottle of Scotch, quarter
filled a glass. He drank. How crucial was the police's concern
about Cane's death? How had they learned it had been he who
had called at Gill Tap that day? What could be the result of their
apparent belief that he had been enjoying an affair? It had seemed
so crucial that they not learn of the friendship, the love, between
them – had that fear been justified? What could he do to salvage
the situation and keep Elaine safe?

He phoned her. 'The police know I've been painting you and
they're—'

'They've been questioning me!'

'I know.'

'They seemed to think something might be wrong.'

'They were obviously suspicious?'

'I'm not certain . . . but they asked me *again* about whether
my marriage was a happy one!'

'What did you say?'

'I told them that . . . I told them that it *had* been happy!'

'But had not been recently?'

'Not in so many words!'

But it was an obvious inference. Linton's heart sank. 'What
else did they ask?'

'About . . . about how his illness had changed him.'

'And you said?'

'Don't interrogate me!' She sounded hysterical.

'I'm sorry. Please forgive me. I just need to know, because
. . .' He trailed off. Would it make her feel worse if she realized
that the police had questioned him?

'Because what?'

He decided that he had to tell her. She had to know that the
police had found out about the portrait he was painting; it would
only make them more suspicious if she denied it when questioned, as he knew she would be. 'It's just . . . A policeman
called at the studio and asked a load of questions about you

and me. He'd somehow tracked me down, so I told him about the portrait that your husband commissioned. I played down our friendship, but he gave the impression he thought we were having an affair.'

'How beastly!'

'As I said the other day, facts can make guilt seem far easier to believe than innocence. We *have* to keep apart until things get cleared up. It's more important now than ever.'

'We can meet somewhere well away.'

'I don't think we dare tempt fate a second time.'

There was a long silence. Then: 'Why are you so afraid?'

'There is a tendency in most people to match facts to a theory.'

'Bingo, guv'nor,' Clements reported cheerfully as he entered Bell's office.

Bell looked up. 'Well?'

Clements did not look deflated by the reception. 'Our Mr Linton is the owner of the rusty Beetle, and he – get this, guv – was *painting Mrs Cane's portrait*. Only, when I entered, I disturbed him creating his art—'

'And?' Bell said, not in the mood for humouring creative storytelling.

'His model was in her birthday suit,' Clements said cheerily, not put off. 'Naked as the day she was born. Not the sort of portrait you'd want to hang in your living room, for fear the mother-in-law would suddenly drop by for tea.'

Bell perked up. 'Nudes, eh?'

Clement nodded. 'Yes, guv. Erotic paintings. Mrs Cane obviously has a saucy side!'

'Did you ask to see the painting of Mrs Cane, to verify it was a nude portrait? He may be a man of many talents.'

Clements' face fell. 'No. Sorry, guv.'

Bell sighed. 'Then get back there immediately and find out.'

Not that a nude portrait was necessarily an indicator of guilt, Bell thought, tapping his pen on his desk as Clements hurried out. But he rather doubted that an aggressive, highly-critical husband on the verge of bankruptcy would have commissioned a nude portrait of his wife.

*   *   *

'Mr Linton? Mr Linton, are you there?'

Linton was jerked out of his reverie. He directed a glare at the staircase. 'Who is it?' he called. He didn't need to ask; it was the police. He knew it in the depth of his being.

'Constable Clements,' the voice called.

'Come on up.'

The policeman appeared; he looked around the room, seemingly disappointed that he wasn't being treated to another eyeful. 'Apologies for disturbing you again, Mr Linton,' he said.

'It's OK,' Linton forced himself to say nonchalantly. 'Happy to help.'

The policeman did not look convinced. 'I wondered if I could see the portrait of Mrs Cane. Just for verification.'

'Don't believe there is one?' Linton asked coldly. He rose and went to the easel that supported the painting, while Clements spluttered a denial. 'Here.'

Clements eyed the painting. 'Very nice,' he said, sounding disappointed.

A dreadful thought crossed Linton's mind. 'You didn't think it was a nude, did you?' he asked.

Clements flushed. 'I didn't like to speculate, Mr Linton.'

Linton endeavoured to scowl. 'A jobbing artist takes the work he can get, Constable Clements. I would prefer to paint respectable portraits only, but that doesn't pay the rent. I was glad to be offered a chance to paint a lady such as Mrs Cane.'

'Of course,' Clements said, not sounding entirely convinced.

'Is that all? Only, I was about to leave my studio for the day,' Linton said.

'Thank you for your help.'

When the policeman had left, Linton stared at the portrait for a while. Elaine was so beautiful; he would have loved to have painted her nude – a classic, tasteful nude – but he wouldn't have been crass enough to suggest it. She knew, of course, what sort of art he made a living from; she didn't judge him for it. She was an understanding woman.

His spirits fell even further as he recalled a perfect afternoon spent in his studio, talking and laughing and sharing secrets. The conversation had turned serious, and she had – and it still excited him to think of the trust she had shown him – lifted up her blouse to show him the faded scar on her stomach. She had, she said, nearly died in an accident. The scar was a reminder to her that life was precious and she should always try to do her best and stay true to her beliefs, whatever the provocation.

That such a wonderful woman might be locked away for some-thing she had not done – would never even have *considered* doing, no matter how badly she was treated – made him more angry and despondent and increased his feeling of hopelessness.

'Sorry, guv. It wasn't a nude. Head and shoulders portrait. Pretty tasteful.'

Bell suppressed a swear word. 'Thank you, Clements.' Blast it! No closer to the truth. But there had to be something fishy about the portrait business. Why would a man who had lost his business, and had the bank on his back, commission such an extravagance? He made a few phone calls. Then he phoned Harmsworth, his superior.

'To keep you in the centre of the picture, sir. We've identified the owner of the car which PC Attwell reported. He is Michael Linton. An artist, hardly known, if at all. PC Clements says his studio is on the top floor of an old flour mill and apparently as bare and cold as an old-fashioned prison cell.'

'Is there a known connection between him and Mrs Cane?'

'He's painting her portrait.'

'Does he admit calling at Gill Tap after Cane died?'

'He denied it until threatened with being identified by PC Attwell.'

'How did he know Cane had died?'

'His story is, he didn't. Only called there because he was afraid she was pretty ill and was worried about possibly losing his fee for the painting.'

'Has there been any suggestion she has not been well recently?'

'No.'

'How did Clements view his evidence?'

'As a pack of feeble lies.'

'Did he challenge Linton over having an affair with Mrs Cane?'

'He thought it better at this stage to take things slowly.'

'Not so slowly they grind along for months.'

'No, sir.'

'Is there any proof pointing to an affair?'

'Nothing sharp.'

'You're presuming there has been one?'

'It seems likely, even though Linton firmly denies he ever meets Mrs Cane outside the studio.'

'Prove that false, or their time together consisted of more than painting, and you think you'll get close to having a case?'

'I'm assuming they were lovers, so it's very likely she panicked after helping her drunken husband sway outwards over the banisters and phoned Linton. I've asked one of the lads to find out what phone calls they've made to each other.'

'That could be an indication, but not much more.'

'Every little indication will help, sir.'

'I'd prefer some hard facts.'

TEN

Lewis looked at his watch. 'I'd better get moving.' He went through to the hall, lifted his mackintosh off the Victorian stand.

Audrey had followed him. 'I hate when you have to work on Sundays. Oh, I've forgotten to tell you. Henry phoned to say he's down this way for a couple of days.'

'What's brought him south?'

'He's going to visit his sister who's in Hopkins Hospital. She's broken her leg. The horse spooked and threw her.'

'Bad luck.'

'He wants to see you. I had a word with mother, and it's OK to invite him to supper. What shall we give him? Would roast chicken be all right?'

'Better lamb chops laced with arsenic.'

'You are quite impossible!'

'Not half as impossible as the sarge will be if I don't get to the station on time.'

She kissed him goodbye.

He drove towards divisional HQ. Henry Killip had been at the training college at the same time as he; they had enjoyed a relationship best described as friendship at arm's length. Killip was self-confident, thrusting, careless of others, a devotee of Aphrodite. He had resigned from the force because of trouble, had worked for a company whose business was of a nature seemingly difficult to describe; Killip had introduced Audrey to him. She had suggested they should ask Killip along for a meal.

'It's a tricky task that faces us,' Bell said as they drove.

'Interviewing Mrs Cane, sir?' Lewis asked. 'Or avoiding Mrs Owen?'

'I don't know why you chose to become a policeman,' Bell said. 'With talent like yours, you could be on the stage. Yes, interviewing Mrs Cane. The noose is tightening, so it is time to bring up the matter of her husband's failing business. I'm particularly keen to know why he would have commissioned a portrait of his dear wife while his finances went tits up.'

'Very droll,' Lewis said dutifully.

'I beg your pardon?'

'I thought you were making a humorous joke, sir,' Lewis said. 'Given that the artist painting her portrait is more accustomed to painting nudes.'

Bell ignored him. 'We must judge whether Mrs Cane knew in advance about her husband's financial trouble, and about the little matter of the insurance policy.'

'Surely any wealthy man keeps a large life insurance policy to benefit his wife should he pass first?' Lewis suggested.

'It must frequently be traumatic to have such a blind faith in the goodness of human nature as yourself?'

Mrs Cane sat very upright on the sofa; there were dark circles under her eyes. Her shadow, Mrs Owen, glowered in the corner.

'Can you tell me about your husband's business, Mrs Cane,' Bell said encouragingly.

'I told you, it's—' Mrs Owen said.

Bell interrupted. 'Mrs Cane?'

'It's a security business,' Mrs Cane said. She sounded very weary. 'They install digital alarms.'

'And is it successful?'

'My husband never involved me in his business affairs. He said a woman's place was in the home.'

Mrs Owen sniffed, audibly, from the corner.

'Did you know, Mrs Cane, that the business was in trouble?'

'I . . . yes.'

'How bad was the trouble?'

She looked down at the floor. 'I . . . I'm not sure,' she said. 'Quite bad, I think.'

'Did you know, Mrs Cane, that your husband had sold the company, prior to his death?'

She nodded.

'Or that the sale of the company was not enough to cover his debts?'

She shook her head.

'I don't wish to alarm you, Mrs Cane, but do you know that this house might have to be sold to cover them?'

Again, she shook her head. But she did not, Bell noted, seem very surprised. There was a kind of lifelessness to her.

'I . . . thought that might be the case,' she offered, after a short silence. 'I knew the trouble was bad, but he would not confide in me.'

'Thank you, Mrs Cane, you've been most helpful,' Bell said. He stood. 'Just one thing before we leave you in peace.'

She did not look up, but Bell thought she flinched.

'Were you aware of any extravagant purchases your husband made before his death?'

Did she relax at that, Bell wondered. Her shoulders dropped, and she looked up. 'No, I don't think so,' she said. 'I . . . I asked him if I could buy an appliance for the kitchen, and he was . . . he was . . .' She stopped and cleared her throat. 'He said no. He told me that he was short of money, had to sell the business and might even have to sell my car.'

'So he would not have bought anything expensive or out of the ordinary?'

'I . . . No,' she faltered. 'I don't think . . .'

'Thank you,' Bell said again.

Back in the car, he turned to Lewis. 'Well?'

'Perhaps the painting was cheap, sir. She might not consider it an extravagant purchase.'

Bell snorted. 'Every cloud has its silver lining, eh? Why do you persist in thinking the good woman is innocent?'

'Because there is no evidence to suggest she *isn't*, sir.'

'Hah!' said Bell. 'In my experience, even a hint of blue sky – there can be some – means there's bound to be rain.'

Elaine picked up the phone and began to dial Mike's number. She shook so much that she could barely see the buttons. Why were the police hounding her? Asking her so many questions? John had had an accident! What did the state of his company matter? She remembered that the policeman had said that she might lose her home . . .

She stood very still for a moment, ordering herself to calm down, face facts, not black imagination. How could the police think she had . . . had . . . *pushed* him?

She had thought Mike was overreacting; she had always presumed that the police would listen to an upright citizen when she told the truth and believe her. But what if they didn't? *What if they thought she had killed him?*

Biting back a sob, she punched in the next digit in Mike's number – then froze. Suddenly, Mike's warning about their not seeing each other made far too much sense. If the police thought that they had been having an affair . . .

Elaine slammed the phone back down. She couldn't put Mike at risk; if the police refused to believe her, they might suspect Mike of wrongdoing too. She couldn't risk dragging him into something so awful. She would have to face it on her own.

'Audrey,' Killip said as he put spoon and fork down on his empty plate, 'we have been dining on nectar.'

'I presume you mean ambrosia.'

'But of course. Trist, old pal, you are in the company of a most intelligent woman; perhaps one day I will enjoy such fortune.'

'Would you consider it good or bad fortune?' she asked.

Killip smirked.

'You'd like coffee?'

'If it's not too much trouble.'

'Only Nescafé.'

'There's nothing nicer.'

'You've actually drunk it?'

He laughed.

As she carried plates into the kitchen, he followed Lewis into the sitting room. 'Nice little home you've got, Trist.' He often used back-praise to hint at his own greater possessions or achievements.

'It belongs to Audrey's parents. I'm a privileged interloper.'

'You're not thinking of buying somewhere?'

'When prices come down, my pay goes up, mortgages are freely available and we're engaged, yes.'

'Tell me, old scout, does Audrey regard me as a bad influence these days?'

'I don't think so.'

'You've not told her too much about the times when we were cadets?'

'No.'

'Remember the two sisters?'

'No.'

'The brunette asked me if you lacked something. Can you guess why?'

'No.'

'It took you days to make a half-hearted pass, and when Marge – or was it Alice? – showed the to-be-expected resistance, you stopped and that was that. It made her think you couldn't be a proper gentleman, even if you normally behaved like one.'

Audrey entered with a tray. Lewis took it from her and, once she was seated, held it so that she could serve herself, then offered it to Killip.

'Audrey,' Killip asked, 'are we permitted to smoke in here?'

'I'd rather you didn't. The parents don't like the smell, and it's so difficult to get rid of.'

'Then I will forgo the vice until later.'

'When it can be enjoyed with other ones?'

Lewis was made uneasy by her sharpness.

'You know, I've been doing so much travelling recently, it's a case of if today is Monday, I'm in Glasgow. If it's Tuesday, I'm in Taunton. Like to do it by car because it's so much more comfortable . . . Did you notice my new toy, Trist?'

'No.'

'Art on the hoof. A Bentley Continental GT. Not many of them around yet.'

'Which, to your pleasure, makes it even more noticeable?' Audrey queried.

'What speed will it do?' Lewis asked hurriedly.

'A couple of hundred.'

'Where the hell can you manage that?'

'Any of the motorways after two in the morning and between speed cameras.' Killip laughed. 'Lower your crime-busting antenna. I've only gone over a hundred and twenty a few times.'

'What on earth is the point of having a car that'll go so ridiculously quickly?' she asked. 'Male ego, I suppose?'

'Why not?'

'Have you had a wander around whilst you've been here?' Lewis asked.

'In-between visits to the hospital. Had clotted cream and strawberry jam at that tea shop in Little Ecton, visited Turnberry House, went over to Devil's Dyke and wondered why. Touch of masochism, most likely.'

'What's that supposed to mean?' she asked.

'I was remembering Penelope and the day we went there and picnicked. It was probably cloudy and cool since it was midsummer, but I remember blue sky and hot sunshine because after the second glass of bubbly she said "yes". I'd forgotten it must have been called the *Devil's* dyke for a reason, though.'

'Did something happen?' Audrey no longer spoke challengingly.

'Shortly afterwards, a drunk driver went into her car and killed her.'

'I . . . I'm so sorry.' She was apologizing for her previous attitude as well as commiserating.

'It's the way life goes.'

'Henry . . .'

'Yes?'

'I'm sure you'll find someone.'

'I hope you're right, because I keep looking, but no one matches you.' He turned and spoke to Lewis. 'Before I push off, how about coming out and having a look at the old jalopy?'

Lewis agreed, even though knowing this would please the other's vanity.

The Bentley was parked immediately outside the house.

'It certainly looks great,' Lewis said.

'Not another car on the road to match it. Forget Ferraris and Lamborghinis – they're for the nouveaux riches.' He opened the driving door. 'It's been great to make contact again, even if things became a bit sticky with your charming fiancée. That's why I reckoned a personal tragedy would warm the atmosphere. In truth, Penelope turned me down and went on to marry a super-market manager who got the sack a year later. Served her right.'

'You lying bastard!'

'Nothing like making a lady sorry for you to get her on your side. Trist, I'm not being pessimistic to suggest you'll fail to make a top spot in the force. Trouble is, you're a naturally decent bloke. So when you're thinking of finding another job, I'll help you land it.'

'And I'll buy one of these?' He indicated the car.

'No offence, but I see you in a Volvo.'

'Dependable, safe and rather dull?'

'Good at staying within the speed limit. And talking of Volvos reminds me. A few days back, I'd met a nice piece. It was unsea-sonably warm, so after lunch at Maison Argent we drove to Devil's Dyke. I was going to go down to The Last Drop – that flat shelf halfway down, by tradition where the devil had a pee, reached by the narrow earth lane that's marked "No Thoroughfare" . . . Know where I mean?'

'Not for the same reason.'

'There was already a car down there – a white Volvo estate.'

'I doubt that proved to be an insurmountable problem to your ambitions.'

'The point is, one of those old Beetles, straight off the scrap heap, passed us and went down there. It drew along the other car, the driver climbed out, a woman came out of the Volvo like a cork out of a champagne bottle, and in a couple of seconds they were so clamped together that if they hadn't been fully dressed, I wouldn't have had to wonder what they were up to. Never before seen anything so erotically unerotic.'

'I've always assumed you've seen and done everything.'

'Still a peak or two to climb.' He opened the driving door.
'Go on chatting and Audrey will worry I've been trying to lead
you astray.'

'I doubt it.'

'So do I. Even the devil in the dyke would have a job to do
that.' He climbed into the car, lowered the window. 'Until we
meet again.'

'I hope your sister is soon better – if you even have a sister
and she's ill, that is!'

Killip drove off with a show of near silent acceleration.

Audrey had remained in the drawing room.

'Audrey . . . You've known Henry for quite some time, haven't
you?' Lewis asked.

'Don't you remember, he introduced us?'

'Was he . . . Did he . . .?'

'You sound very uncertain! Has Henry made you jealous of
his new car, which can overtake light?'

'Of course not.'

'Something must be wrong when you deny that as if you'd
been accused of swindling old ladies.'

'I . . .'

'Spit it out, but not too closely.'

Her teasing manner made it even more difficult to put the
question which was savaging his mind.

She stood, went to where he stood, took hold of his hands.
'Tell me.'

'How well . . . How well did you know Henry before he
introduced you to me?' he asked in a rush of words.

'Why d'you ask?'

'Just wondered.'

'Wondered what?'

'Nothing.'

'Nothing has made you . . .?' She studied him intently. 'You
wonder if maybe I knew him *very* well?'

He looked away from her.

'You want to know if we "ran a course" together?'

He shook his head.

'We've promised never to lie to each other, yet I'm sure you've
just lied. Perhaps you think he came here hoping he'd have the

chance to continue; that I'd be so dazzled by him and his car, the huge house he's bought with an Olympic size swimming pool, I'd drive off into the sunset with him?'

He dared not answer.

'He is a smooth, self-centred, self-promoting fantasist who's convinced he's irresistible to women. That amused me in a strange sort of way, which is why I remained friendly with him; when it became necessary, I told him I had no wish or intention of becoming his umpteenth victim and the man I loved would have to love me for myself, not because of his bed rating. He said I was demanding a man who could cartwheel on water. No doubt his amour propre very soon repaired itself. When I next saw him, he was friendly, but nothing more. No wandering hands, no suggestion of a trip to Monte Carlo. And when he introduced you to me, I knew I'd found the man who metaphorically *could* cartwheel on water.'

'I . . . just the way . . . what he said . . . I'm sorry.'

'So you damned well should be!' She lessened her condemnation by loving words in-between kissing him.

Lewis entered Hopkins' office. 'Sarge, what car does Mrs Cane drive?'

'Don't think it's on the records. Why the interest?'

'An old acquaintance, Henry Killip, came to supper with Audrey last night. We were at police college together, but he quit the force and went into some sort of business which must—'

'Skip the history.'

'He went up to Devil's Dyke with a woman. A very battered Beetle went past them and down to The Last Drop – you know where I mean?'

'Having lived here for umpteen years, I've an idea.'

'A white Volvo was already down there, and the Beetle went down, parked alongside it. A woman came out of the Volvo and went into a very amorous clinch with the Beetle owner.'

'When was this?'

'A few days ago, which would make it midweek.'

'The time?'

'I imagine it was midday to early afternoon.'

'Did he see either of them clearly enough to be able to identify them?'

'He wouldn't have been able to from the top. But maybe he got a reasonable look at the driver of the Beetle as it went past.'

'Did he get either of the cars' numbers?'

'I don't know.'

'Why not?'

'I didn't ask because . . . Things were a bit disturbed, and it was only after he'd driven off, I realized there might be something in what he'd told me.'

'Ever late. Ring your friend and find out all you can.'

'It'll take a bit of time because he doesn't live locally and I'm not certain where he's staying. Probably in a hotel . . .'

'Then ring hotels!'

Hopkins followed Lewis out, but turned right and went into the DI's room.

'Unless someone's under armed siege,' Bell said, 'it'll have to wait.'

'I think you'll find it worthwhile listening to, sir.'

'You've got ten seconds.'

'I've just had Lewis along. A friend of his was at Devil's Dyke and saw a white Volvo and a battered Beetle together. A woman from the Volvo and a man from the Beetle went into a passionate clinch. Lewis was in some sort of private trouble and didn't immediately realize the possible significance of what he'd been told, which is why it's taken time for him to report.'

'Any other details?'

'None. His friend didn't name precise date, time or note car numbers, has never met Mrs Cane or Linton.'

'You've told Lewis to question his friend to find out?'

'Yes, sir.' Hopkins was briefly annoyed he should be asked that. 'But Lewis doesn't know where the friend is staying, and until we find out, there's not much we can do.'

'Sir,' Bell said, speaking to the detective chief superintendent over the phone, 'we may have uncovered a promising lead in the Cane case.'

'You have or you haven't?'

Harmsworth's manner suggested things weren't running smoothly at county HQ. 'I'm afraid I can't say yet.'

'It would have been better to make certain before phoning.'

'The way things have gone, it seemed better to tell you . . .'

The call ended ten minutes later. Why, Bell wondered as he replaced the receiver, did seniors not have the wit to accept events never ran as smoothly as hoped?

'County Hotel.'

'Do you have a Mr Killip staying there?' Lewis asked, after stating his name and occupation.

'One moment.'

He looked at the newspaper on his desk. The salary of the chairman of the local council was twenty thousand pounds a year more than the prime minister's. Abolish both positions and there would be more money for those whose jobs mattered.

The receptionist said: 'Mr Killip was a guest here only until earlier this morning.'

'Did he say where he was going?'

'There is no record that he did.'

'Did he give an address when he registered?'

'Yes.'

'Will you give it to me?'

'I'm sure you'll understand that we are not obliged to demand proof that the address given is correct.'

'That would be bad for trade?'

There was silence.

'Would you give it to me, please?'

'Risdome House, Upper Aichen, Hants.'

'Do you have a phone number?'

'No.'

Lewis thanked the other, thanks not acknowledged, phoned the cheapest firm providing enquiries. They gave the required number. He dialled it.

'Is Mr Killip there?' he asked.

'I regret he is not at home,' answered a woman in a cut-glass accent.

Bitchily superior, he judged. He should have realized that Killip would be married. While very useful socially to Killip, she no doubt despised his lack of aristocratic blood, his manners and amours, but his money enabled her to endure them. 'Will you ask him—'

'Who is speaking?'

'Detective Constable Lewis.'

'Why do you wish to speak to him?'

'To ask him about something.'

'And what would that be?'

'I'll explain to him.'

She put her phone down.

In the old days, Killip had called his briefly entertained companions 'Pleasure Girls'. Lewis wondered what in private he called his wife.

Killip rang as Lewis was about to leave divisional HQ and return home. 'What's the panic, Trist? Handed in your resignation and would like a job starting at fifty Ks?'

'I need more information on the Volvo and Beetle you saw at Devil's Dyke.'

'Why the curiosity?'

'They may have been driven by people we're interested in. When precisely did you see them, date and time?'

'You'll accept the word of a lying bastard?'

'You may be able to tell the truth occasionally.'

Killip laughed. 'Depends if that's profitable.'

'When?'

'Four or five days ago.'

'Which?'

'If I can remember the name of the woman I had—'

'Messalina?'

'Too free with her favours.'

'You mentioned lunch at Maison Argent.'

'That's it! She was a nice piece, but the lunch was divine. I called in at Burgomeisters to see the boss man. He was away, so I had a chat with his PR man, met . . . Angela, I think her name was . . . in the office, and she thought lunch at Maison Argent would be fun. After a bottle of Krug and one of Romany something-or-other, we went for a drive.'

'On which day did you go to burgomaster?'

'Burgo*meister*. No relation to the law. It was Thursday.'

'At what time were you at Devil's Dyke?'

'Not long before dark.'

'Did you notice any part of the registration number of either car?'

'I had too much on my hands to do so.'

'Could you see the driver of the Beetle sufficiently well to be able to recognize him?'

'No.'

'The woman in the Volvo?'

'She had everything in its right place, but that's all.'

'You said they greeted each other enthusiastically.'

'Like they'd been dry for a couple of years.'

'How long were they there?'

'You think I'd be bothered to stay around to see what happened next?'

'You were in a hurry to cash in on what you'd spent on your pleasure girl?'

'You've become nasty-minded.'

The telephone rang; Hopkins answered the call with a 'good morning'.

'You've requested a full report on calls made between two numbers?'

'That's right.'

'We need to fax or email the list – far too long to give over the phone.'

'Fax will be safer; someone here always presses the wrong tit on the computer.'

Twenty-five minutes later, Hopkins entered the DI's room.

'Yes?' demanded Bell testily.

'This has come in from the telephone people, sir.' He passed across three sheets of paper. 'I've marked the ones from Gill Tap to Linton in red, from Linton to Gill Tap in yellow.'

'You've confirmed Linton doesn't have a mobile?'

'Yes. Probably too expensive a luxury for him.'

Bell studied the lists, opened one of the files on his desk, brought out several sheets of paper, compared details in them with the dates he had just been given. 'There was a call from Mrs Cane to Linton very shortly before she reported the death of her husband. So Linton almost certainly knew about the death when he called at the house on the pretext of her recent ill health. After a couple more calls, there was a brief silence. Thursday, there was a long call from Mrs Cane to Linton in the afternoon. Thursday afternoon is when there was the sighting of a white Volvo and a decrepit Beetle at the Devil's Dyke. I think we can accept, but cannot yet prove, she was desperate to meet him and they arranged the meeting.'

'Maybe can't prove it, sir, but when one looks at all the facts and notes how they meld in, the picture is clear.'

'The DCS is no lover of probabilities and suppositions, any more than is the CPS.'

'Facts are facts.'

'Their interpretations aren't.' Bell looked at his watch. 'Have you any idea whether Linton is likely to be at the studio?'

'I'm afraid I don't know. Artists' lifestyles aren't my speciality.'

'Nor mine, but I'd rather a fruitless visit than one he's prepared for.'

'It could make for an interesting visit if he's doing one of his eyeball paintings.'

'He paints eyeballs?'

'Evocatively positioned ladies in the buff.'

'At my age they begin to evoke nostalgia rather than lust. I'll want someone with me, and I'll leave in a quarter of an hour.'

'I'll tell Lewis.'

'Then have a quiet word with him and explain I do not believe in poetic faith.'

'I'm not certain I understand, sir.'

'A constant suspension of disbelief.'

ELEVEN

Linton was adding a final touch to an experimental still life when there was a call from street level. He shouted a reply, went to the head of the stairs.

Bell introduced Lewis. Linton hoped his uneasiness was not obvious. This further visit from the police must mean they were not satisfied by what they had been told by Elaine or him.

In their minds, tuned to guilt, it probably seemed likely she had had some part in her husband's death. That she had, perhaps, pushed her husband off the balcony so she could be with her lover. The possibility/probability she had had an adulterous relationship with him *had* to be refuted.

'Sorry to barge in like this,' Bell said. 'I'm hoping you can give us a little time.'

'I'll move the chairs. They're slightly more comfortable than standing.' He placed the only two in the studio near to the bed, sat on the edge of that.

Bell spoke in a friendly manner. 'We're trying to sort out a problem or two which have arisen over Mr Cane's unfortunate death and hope you'll be able to help us.'

'I'll certainly do so if I can, but I doubt I'll be successful.'

'How long have you known Mr and Mrs Cane?'

'I suppose it's a few months since he asked me to paint his wife.'

'You were not friendly with him before that?'

'No. I met him at a cocktail party. It was then that he asked me to paint his wife's portrait.'

'Was his wife there?'

'Yes.'

'You thought she'd be a suitable subject?'

Linton managed a smile. 'Inspector, for a painter like me, there is no such person as an unsuitable subject.'

'You're not quite as successful as you'd like?'

'Is anyone?'

'Where did you paint her?'

'Here.'

'Did she come frequently to be painted?'

'Fairly often.'

'It was taking a long time to paint her?'

'If a portrait is to be any good, it usually does. The inner character is difficult to fix.'

'You're in danger of becoming too arty for us, but can you say what you perceived her inner character to be?'

'Warm, sympathetic, faithful.' Linton did not think it would do any harm to put stress on the word 'faithful'.

'You developed a friendship with her?'

'As one tries to do with one's sitter.'

'Did it become a personal friendship?'

'An impersonal one.'

'Did you not sometimes go out with her for a coffee or a drink when you'd finished work?'

Linton felt on safe ground here. There was no evidence that he'd ever done so, surely? 'No.'

'You were careful to keep the relationship a purely professional one?'

'Naturally.'

'Then you have never been in her company except here, in this studio?'

'That's right.'

'Do you sometimes phone her at her home?'

Linton thought quickly. Would the police be able to provide any evidence to prove the calls between them? They had not been all *that* numerous; Elaine was ever wary of her husband's temper. 'Only if I need to cancel a sitting. I don't think that's happened more than a couple of times.'

'And if there's a reason, she phones you?'

'Such as when she had a bad cold, she couldn't come for a while and kept me informed as to when she hoped to be back.'

'She phoned you only on such occasions?'

'As I remember.'

'You appear to have a poor memory.'

'What d'you mean?' Linton knew he had spoken too sharply. Nerves were threatening his attempt to remain calm, perplexed, but unworried by their visit.

'Mrs Cane phoned you very shortly before she phoned the police to report her husband's death.'

The phone call suggested a prearranged plot, not the reality – panic threatened to take away all power to reason. Never mind the facts, he would deny it. 'If she thinks she did, she's wrong.'

'We have obtained a list of all calls from her to you and you to her over a considerable period. They have been what we would describe as frequent.'

Linton's growing uneasiness became fear.

'Was her call on Tuesday to tell you her husband had suffered a fatal fall in their house?'

'No.'

'It was made at ten past five. Evidence suggests he died earlier that afternoon, after a physical fight with Mrs Cane.' Bell spoke in the same even tone.

Sharp fear became panic.

'Previously, you have denied any knowledge of Mr Cane's death until you learned about it when you visited Gill Tap.'

He struggled to regain mental coherence. 'Are you trying to confuse me?'

'Why should I do that?'

'Because you seem to think I've been lying.'

'It would seem you have been.'

'Mrs Cane did phone me. She was in a terrible state and said she had returned home after being away a short while and found her husband had fallen and seemed to be dead. She asked me what to do.'

'What was your advice?'

'To ring the family doctor immediately.'

'Why did she seek your advice when, as you have told us, your relationship was purely on a professional level?'

'How do you expect me to be able to answer that?'

'Do you own a car?'

The change in direction of the questioning made Linton desperately try to judge why. 'Yes.'

'Is it an old Volkswagen Beetle in poor condition?'

'Yes.'

'There has been no change of ownership notified to the licensing authorities.'

'Then that's somehow been forgotten.'

'You would appear to be of a forgetful nature. Did you drive anywhere on Thursday?'

The reason for their interest in the car sharply became clear. He remembered Elaine's frantic need for his moral support, his reluctant agreement to meet her. He had thought solitude would ensure their meeting would go unrecorded; he should have remembered the safest place to hide was in a crowd.

'Did you?' Bell expressed no irritation at the lack of an answer.

Linton panicked further, did not know what to say, attempted to dissemble. 'I can't remember.'

'Let me refresh your memory. You drove to Devil's Dyke.'

'Where?' A mistake, Linton thought as soon as he'd said it. It was unlikely that, as a local, he would not have heard of Devil's Dyke.

A shout from below interrupted the questioning. 'Are you there? And it ain't no good saying you ain't.'

'Who is it?' Bell asked irritably. He had had Linton on the run, and the interruption had broken the feeling of inevitable failure which the other had begun to suffer.

'The rent collector.'

A large man with a shaved head, an expression of mindless aggression, reached the top of the stairs and stepped into the studio. He looked at Bell, quickly away.

'As you can see,' Linton said, 'I have visitors. Perhaps you could come back tomorrow?'

'No, squire, I bloody can't.' His voice was as rough as his appearance. 'There are too many tomorrows from you. You're three months overdue, and Mr Harfing told you last month that if you didn't cough up the next rent day, he'd have you out on your arse.'

Linton went over to the changing-room, returned with a large wad of bank notes which he gave to Weekes, who counted and recounted them, tongue constantly running along his upper lip. He pocketed the money, began to leave.

'I'd like a receipt.'

Weekes brought a scrumpled form and a ballpoint pen out of his pocket, signed his name with some difficulty. He handed the receipt to Linton, slouched across to the stairs, left.

'Didn't know he'd become a rent collector,' Bell remarked. 'Mr Linton, you won't want us around any longer than we have to be, so we'll move on ASAP. You were saying you don't know where Devil's Dyke is?'

'The name didn't immediately mean anything,' he prevaricated.

'But it does now? Do you agree you drove there last Thursday?'

'No.'

'Did you meet Mrs Cane there?'

'No.'

'A white Volvo was seen on the shelf of land which is sometimes called The Last Drop. What car does she drive?'

'I don't know.'

'Strange! A white Volvo estate. A Volkswagen Beetle, as close to scrap metal as possible when it can still move, went down to the shelf. Was that your car?'

'It's not the only ancient Beetle still on the road.'

'Quite possibly, but that does not answer the question.'

Temper got the better of him. 'Which you have silently and incorrectly answered because you believe it was my car and I met Mrs Cane.'

'A policeman from another division saw you arrive, noted your car because of its appearance. He has identified you as the driver of it.'

'How?'

'By eyesight.'

'He knows me?'

'He didn't. Having been shown a photo of you, he identified you.'

'Who showed him the photograph?'

'I did.'

'Where did you get it?'

'Once I became aware the relationship between Mrs Cane and you might be stronger than you would admit, I arranged for one of my lads to take it.'

Bell's lies – exaggerations, as he would no doubt describe them – worried Lewis. In his naivety, he believed a policeman should not use lies.

'This officer, there on a picnic, watched the car park alongside a white Volvo estate. A lady came out of the Volvo and you and she embraced with considerable passion.'

'What was the number of the Volvo?' Linton tried to turn the interrogation on its head.

'The officer was not on duty and had no reason at the time to take the number.'

Linton pressed his advantage. 'Then you can only say it was a white Volvo. There must be thousands of such cars. What was the number of the Beetle?'

'I do not have it, but would you claim your Beetle in its present condition is not unique?'

Linton thought about that, decided that the police could prove he was there, but had no evidence that his companion was Mrs Cane. 'I accept it was me. I met a friend whom I'd not been able to see for quite some time.'

'Mrs Cane phoned you shortly before you met.'

'To explain she would not, naturally, be able to come to the studio for some time.'

'Very well.' Bell stood. 'Before we leave, would you allow us to see your portrait of Mrs Cane?'

He showed them the portrait. They made the required complimentary comments.

Bell and Lewis left, drove from the old mill in the direction of the centre of town.

'Did you recognize the rent collector?' Bell asked.

'No, sir,' Lewis replied.

'I've seen him before, but can't place when or where. It'll come in its own good time. One thing I am certain is at that time he was collecting betting debts, not rents, and all paid up smartly or visited a hospital.'

Lewis braked to a halt for a red light. 'That was a great painting of Mrs Cane.'

'Was it?'

'You didn't think so, sir?'

'Looked like her, but isn't that what a portrait's supposed to do?'

'It made me think of what he said earlier about needing to find the inner character of the sitter.'

'Artistic tripe. Picasso found inner characters with several heads and triangular noses.'

'I reckon Linton found Mrs Cane's.'

'How do you see them?'

Lewis did not answer. He had seen honesty, loyalty and love, but her love would be construed as guilt because it had become accepted that where there was love, there was sex.

The lights changed, and they drove past one of the hypermarkets responsible for the lack of small, family-owned shops in town.

'We could have continued on and questioned Mrs Cane again,' Bell said, half speaking to himself, 'but he will have phoned seconds after we left, and she'll have had time to think up answers. And there's nothing like waiting to rattle the nerves.'

They reached divisional HQ, parked in the DI's allotted bay. Lewis pressed down his door handle.

'Hang on.'

He released the handle.

'How much money did Linton hand the rent man?'

'Can't rightly say.'

'If I could remember the man's name . . . Weekes, by God! That's the name of the rent collector. So he can . . .' He did not finish the sentence. If Weekes was to be 'persuaded' to provide what evidence he could, he would need to be under greater pressure than Lewis would probably impose. 'Tell Morgan to gen up on Weekes' history – he'll have form – and then find out how much cash Linton gave him. A month's rent for a dump like that won't add up to much, so, as Weekes made clear, Linton can't have paid for a good few months. Even so, where did he find the money?'

'He must get paid for his naked women.'

'Enough to live on, pay the rent for his apartment and still come up with a good few hundred, just like that? Tell Morgan to go to Mr and Mrs Cane's bank, speak to the manager and find out what withdrawals she and Mr Cane made in the past weeks.'

The ringing continued. Linton had the frightening thought that the tension had become too great for Elaine . . .

'Yes?' she said listlessly.

'It's Mike. I've just had a couple of detectives asking more questions.'

'Why can't they understand—'

He cut into what she had been going to say. 'They know you phoned me before you reported John's death.'

'How can they?'

'They've records of all the calls between us.'

'Oh, God!' she murmured.

'Someone saw us at Devil's Dyke.'

'But you said the police could never have known about it!'

'I was as wrong as one can be. They're not saying anything definite, but it's very obvious they think you may have had some part in John's death.'

'How can they, when I didn't?' Hysteria was rising in her voice.

'They're bound to question you again.'

'I can't stand it all. I can't!'

He wanted to be with her, give her strength, knew he daren't. 'If they ask you whether you made certain telephone calls, make them identify them. Deny that when you phoned me on Thursday, we arranged to meet at Devil's Dyke. When they assert you were there in the Volvo, tell them that's nonsense. If they allege you and I embraced on the Last Drop, deny it very strongly: they didn't get the number of the Volvo or any description of the driver. Say that if it was my Beetle, I must have been with some other woman. When they question you again about Tuesday, just repeat the truth.'

'I . . . I'll never remember all that. We've got to be together so you can tell me.'

'We daren't take the risk.'

'Mike, why won't you understand what it's like for me, on my own?'

'I do, but it would be fatal to be seen together again.'

'We can drive to somewhere where no one can possibly know us. Please, Mike!'

'What's happened proves it's impossible to be completely safe.'

'I'm . . . I'm so frightened. If I don't see you . . .'

He managed to persuade her that however bitter their present situation, if they remained apart and provided the police with no further evidence to suggest a much closer relationship existed between them, the wild accusations, the wrong inferences, must eventually be seen as nonsense.

TWELVE

Carter-Johnson was well liked by his superiors because he never questioned the logic of their orders, treated them with the respect they considered they deserved, lacked the ambition to seek further promotion and so offered no threat to those who sought, or had, high positions in the bank company.

Seated at his desk, on which was a computer and printer, geometrically arranged, papers likewise, he said: 'A regular amount was drawn each week by Mr Cane.'

'During how long a period?'

'For many months.'

'How did he take it?'

'An old-fashioned method. He cashes a cheque on his personal account.'

'No out-of-kilter withdrawals?'

'I was about to deal with that.'

Carter-Johnson amused Morgan. The traditional (but perhaps extinct) black coat and striped trouser English white collar worker: bustling, nervous, never without bowler hat and rolled umbrella, a popular subject for cartoons.

'Unusually, Mr Cane withdrew a considerably larger sum just over a week ago. That is to say, nine hundred pounds.'

'Cash?'

'Yes.'

'What about Mrs Cane's account?'

Carter-Johnson brought up another page of figures on the computer screen. 'Her account is small and infrequently activated; we maintain it only because of her husband's accounts.'

'You only rob the rich?'

'That is supposed to be amusing, Constable?'

Morgan was unfazed by the implied rebuke. 'Did you cash the cheque for nine hundred?'

'A clerk naturally did so.'

'I'd like to talk to whoever it was.'

'If you must.' Carter-Johnson spoke over the internal telephone to one person, then to a second.

They waited, neither enjoying any degree of harmony with the other.

There was a knock on the door; a woman in her early thirties entered.

'This . . . detective wishes to have a word with you, Miss Harbert. Please sit down.'

He had almost made the mistake of saying 'this gentleman',

Morgan decided. He watched her sit. Remove the glasses, add some make-up, find a dress with some sparkle and she could have a man walking, if not running. 'I've a cousin called Harbert. The family came out to Australia in the nineteenth century, but it was after transportation finished, so if any of them was a crook, they hadn't been caught.'

'Interesting,' Carter-Johnson said disparagingly. 'Miss Harbert has a considerable amount of work to complete, so would you be as brief as possible?'

'I'll keep off all the long words I don't understand. Miss Harbert, do you know John Cane?'

'Yes. Which is to say, he often came to the bank and frequently to my till.'

'Just over a week ago, he cashed—'

'A week and a *half* ago,' Carter-Johnson corrected.

Morgan added: 'At ten thirty-two and forty-three seconds.'

She managed to subdue a smile.

'The cheque was for nine hundred pounds—'

'On his private, not business account,' Carter-Johnson interrupted.

'Do you remember him doing so?' Morgan asked.

'Yes. But it wasn't him who offered it,' she answered.

'Who was it, then?'

'His wife. I would have honoured the cheque immediately if I hadn't noticed the signature was not his usual one. Mrs Cane explained he was not well and his hands were shaky.'

'She had the right to sign his cheques?'

Carter-Johnson answered. 'I had suggested it would be advisable if he gave her such right, since one cannot be certain about the future, and were he unable to sign his cheques, especially those on the company's accounts, it would save considerable trouble if he gave her the right – in her own name, of course – but he refused.'

'Reckoned she'd go on a spending warpath?'

Carter-Johnson sniffed his disapproval.

'Do you know why he wanted the extra money?'

'I did not speak to him. Had I done so, I should not have posed such a question.'

Morgan twirled hairs on his right-hand sideburn. 'I'd like to see the specimen signature he'll have given you and that's in the files.'

'I'm sorry that I . . .' she began, then stopped. Noticing Carter-Johnson's expression, she defended herself. 'After all, I knew she was his wife, so I thought—'

'The wife's rights must never be assumed, Miss Harbert.'

'Unlike the husband's?' Morgan suggested.

'If you will leave with Miss Harbert, Constable, she will provide you with what you want.'

The CID car came to a halt in front of Gill Tap.

Bell remarked: 'A historic old cottage ruined.'

'If the inside's comfortable, that's OK by me, sir,' Clements said as he switched off the engine. 'But the wife wouldn't be seen dead in it.'

'An unfortunate expression in the circumstances . . . What would be her objection?'

'Reckons the older the house, the more people have lived in it – and if any of 'em had unhappy lives, it'll be an unhappy house.'

'Then only a newly built one carries a guarantee of happiness?'

'I don't try to argue with her.'

'The recipe for a happy marriage. We'll go in and try to learn more about an *un*happy marriage.'

Maggie Owen opened the front door. She said angrily: 'Haven't you lot upset her enough?'

'I am afraid we must ask Mrs Cane a few more questions,' Bell answered.

'How would you like to be bothered day after day?'

'I assure you we would not be here unless there was no option.'

Reluctantly, she stepped back to let them enter the hall. She shut the door behind them with unnecessary force. 'You'll have to wait. She's upstairs.'

'If you would ask her to come down—'

'She'll do that in her own good time. Best go in there.' With a wave of her hand, she indicated the sitting-room door; this time she was not even offering the politeness of showing them in.

At Bell's lead, they sat. On a table were magazines and the

week's edition of the local newspaper. Bell picked up a copy of *Country Life* and read the advertisements of large estates for sale; Clements studied the advertisements in the local paper of small houses on the outskirts of the town.

Elaine entered. They came to their feet, replaced newspaper and magazine.

'I'm sorry to have to trouble you again . . .' Bell began.

'But could not miss the chance?' She sat. Grief had turned to truculence, Bell thought.

'You will know I've very recently spoken to Mr Linton.'

'Why should I?'

'I imagine he phoned you very soon after we left him yesterday.'

'Your imagination has raced since my husband died.'

'I have to consider all possibilities.'

'But prefer impossibilities. Why can't you understand I've told you the truth?'

'I will do so when I have confirmed it *is* the truth. Some of the questions I shall be asking, I will have asked before. I hope you will bear with the repetition.'

'Do I have an option? John was nastily drunk. He attacked me before I managed to get out of the house. I returned, hoping he would have calmed down, found him in . . . in the hall.'

A rehearsed tale? 'Mr Linton will have explained we have a record of all phone calls between you and him. You phoned him very shortly after you discovered your husband had fallen. Why was that?'

'I was shocked and needed help.'

'It did not occur to you to contact Mr Cane's doctor or an emergency service?'

'I couldn't think straight.'

'In your confusion, you believed Mr Linton was the most likely to be able to help you?'

Her self-control wavered. 'Y–yes.'

'Why?'

Self-possession returned. She sat up very straight. 'He'll always help someone if he can.'

'You are very friendly with him?'

'Just friendly.'

'You see him often?'

'When I go to his studio for him to paint me.'

'Not on any other occasion? There is no friendly relationship?'

'No.' A firm reply. Bell decided to try a different tack.

'Did your husband like Mr Linton?'

'He was told Mike was a good painter and commissioned him. I doubt he liked or disliked Mike.'

'You use his Christian name.' A slip-up?

'Is that unusual in this day and age? Do you expect us to have addressed each other as Mr and Mrs while he painted me? Or do you somehow manage to think that has some significant meaning?'

'You own a white Volvo estate?'

'I . . . no.'

'I understand you do.'

'It is . . . It was my husband's.'

'You do not have your own car?'

'He had to sell it.'

'Have you driven the Volvo in the past eight days?'

'Yes.'

'Where to?'

'The shops, the countryside, to a friend; anywhere to get a couple of hours away.'

'To Devil's Dyke?'

'No.'

'You have not recently driven there in the Volvo?'

'I've just said not.'

'You are quite certain?'

'Why do you disbelieve everything I say?'

'I need to test your evidence.'

'Why?'

'You had a sharp argument with your husband—'

'You *told* me I had.'

'I will rephrase that. In the light of the evidence, you agreed you had had an argument with him just before his tragic death. What was that argument about?'

'I can't remember.'

'In the circumstances, that seems a little difficult to believe.'

'If you had been attacked by a drunken man, broken free, left the house, returned to find he had fallen and was a bloody mess, you'd forget a lot of things.'

'Mrs Cane, did you cash a cheque for nine hundred pounds a week and a half ago?'

'Yes,' she murmured after a long pause.

'What did you need the money for?'

'Housekeeping.'

'Did your husband normally cash a cheque for housekeeping each week?'

'Yes.'

'For a considerably smaller sum?'

'Yes.'

'So it was unusual for you to go to the bank to draw that money on his behalf?'

'I did so when he was too busy.'

'Why did he draw much more than normal when his finances were in an unfortunate state?'

'I don't know.'

'Was this money in his possession at the time of his death?'

'I've no idea.'

'You have not found such a sum in the house?'

'He must have spent it.'

'Did he often draw reasonably large sums of money without your being aware of what he spent it on?'

'Sometimes.'

'His accounts show this did not happen.'

She was silent.

'Were you aware that Mr Linton had been threatened with eviction from his studio if he did not pay the overdue rent?'

'No.'

'He never mentioned that fact to you?'

'No. And I should not expect him to.'

'This morning, Mr Linton was able to pay his back-rent. It totalled just short of nine hundred pounds.'

Her fingers whitened as she increased the pressure with which she gripped her hands together.

'Did you give Mr Linton the nine hundred pounds you with-drew from the bank?'

'No.'

'You will appreciate then that the coincidence seems rather far-fetched. In truth, I think you withdrew the money without your husband's authority, that he became alerted to the fact on the day of his death, and that in his drunken state he accused you of stealing the money and became violent.'

'The argument had nothing to do with money.'

'How can you be so certain when you've told me you can't remember what it was about?'

She stood, ran out of the room.

Bell, followed by Clements, walked to the doorway, turned into the hall to face Mrs Owen.

'Clear off,' she said violently.

THIRTEEN

Weekes was noted in Records as a habitué of the Crown Jewels. He was also known as a villain's best friend, though not so obviously, because the owner of the pub had so far acted as a receiver with sufficient skill to have escaped exposure to the police or severe injury from a dissatisfied customer. He had a weightlifter's frame and muscle; his wife had a bitter tongue and an encyclopedic knowledge of whom had carried out the most recently profitable heist.

Morgan's entry into the bar caused confused doubt. In a company in which one man had done time for murder, one for intent to murder, three had had heavy sentences for grievous bodily harm, others had records for lesser offences and their women matched them in character and sometimes violence, a policeman was not expected to enter when on his own.

'George Weekes?' Morgan called out.

All talking had ceased. They stared at him, their hatred evident. Two facts restrained their violence: Morgan's aggressive self-confidence, and their certainty that there must be a squad outside, waiting to rush in and arrest everyone for whom there was reasonable cause for doing so. This covered the majority of those present.

Morgan brought a photograph out of his coat pocket, studied it, slowly looked at the customers. His gaze fixed on one man. 'Care for a word, George?'

Those standing too near Weekes moved away.

Morgan put the question in front of them all, knowing that if he called the other outside, Weekes would say nothing, scared of its being thought he had grassed on someone. 'You've been collecting overdue rent from an unhappy punter who paints in the old mill. How much did you take him for?'

Weekes considered the question.

'Maybe you'd rather come down to the factory to talk about it?'

'Nine hundred,' he finally said.

Morgan left. Weekes was questioned about what had taken place; his explanation that they knew as much as he did was treated with jeers. But since it seemed no harm would come to anyone present, the question was dropped and the drinking continued.

Bell, seated at his desk, yawned. He and Susan had sat up into the early hours of the morning, waiting for their daughter to return home. That had caused a row with Vivien, and when finally in bed, he had been unable to fall asleep quickly. Vivien had reacted with teenage anger. Did they think she was acting like a tart just because she didn't return home when they thought she should? Then she'd behave like one in order not to disappoint them! Neither he nor his wife believed they should control a daughter's lifestyle, but they—

'Morning, guv'nor,' Morgan said cheerfully as he entered.

'Do daughters in Australia reckon their fathers are old busybodies?'

'If they know who their fathers are.'

'You bring a different outlook to life.'

Morgan waited, then said: 'I had a chat with Weekes yesterday evening as you asked guv. Weekes told me the amount due on the rent was nine hundred quid. You'll remember that's the amount of the cheque Mrs Cane cashed.'

'Yes.' Bell spoke sharply to make it clear his mind had not been occupied with other subjects. 'Did you think to ask for a copy of his authenticated signature from the bank?'

'Here, sir.' Morgan passed the cheque and a photocopy across the desk.

Bell placed the signature on the cheque immediately above the specimen one. 'Not two peas in a pod.'

'Ten to one, it's slush.'

'Get these to Forensics . . . Paying off his debts is going to prove a boomerang for her.'

'They were used for knocking birds out of the sky rather than returning to hand after being thrown.'

'I'm grateful for the correction.'

Linton accepted he would be questioned again. He had tried and failed to think up credible answers to the likely questions. When he heard the footsteps of two men climbing the stairs up to the studio, he childishly wished for something, somebody, to save him from what was to come.

Elaine had called him, distraught, and what he had learned had sent him to the depths of despair. He had known that her husband had been unpleasant and violent, and that he had drunk both hard and often; had wished it were not so with all his heart. But he had not known that the man's incompetence had all but ruined him, threatening to drag his lovely wife down with him.

If had known, he would never have allowed Elaine to lend him the money for the rent. She had assured him that £900 was but a small sum, easily spared by a husband who paid little attention to his accounts . . .

She had not told the truth.

Now these policemen, with their suspicious minds and inability to see what was so obvious to him – that Elaine was a noble, selfless, self-sacrificing, faithful woman – would draw a poisonous conclusion: that Elaine had stolen money from her husband to help her lover.

The noose was tightening round her neck, and Linton could think of nothing he could do to make the police believe the truth.

Bell and Lewis entered, wished him a good morning. Bell, in friendly fashion, asked him to forgive this further intrusion. They would be grateful if he would help them clear up a problem or two that had turned up. They sat – the two detectives on chairs, Bell on the bed.

'When we were last here,' Bell said, 'a rent collector turned up and demanded you pay the rent due for this studio, adding that if you did not, the owner of the property would, as he put it, have you out on your arse. Have I recalled events correctly?'

'Near enough.'

'You paid the rent then and there.'

'Yes.'

'How much was it?'

'A few hundred. I don't remember exactly.'

'The receipt you were given will answer that.'

'I don't know what I did with it.'

'Poor memories feature largely in this enquiry. I can tell you, it was for nine hundred pounds.'

'Yes, of course.'

'Are you earning a healthy income from your painting?'

'It is not obvious that I do not?'

'Do you have a part-time job which enables you to augment your painting income?'

'No.'

'Then one has to wonder how you managed to pay the nine hundred pounds?'

'I live very simply, which enables me to save a little each week and then be able to meet the rent.'

'The rent collector mentioned you were months overdue, which suggests that for some time you failed to do so.'

If only he had not accepted the money . . . Surely, it would have been better to have lost his studio than to have put Elaine in this intolerable position. 'I'd helped an old friend, which left me short of money,' he lied, unable to think of a more convincing excuse. If he told the truth – that he had simply not sold enough paintings recently and so could not afford to pay the rent – the police would point to his previous ability to pay and be unconvinced.

'What do you mean by the phrase "helped an old friend"?'

'We met, and he was so downcast, I asked him what was the problem. He said he was in debt to someone who was violent when debts were not repaid on the dot.'

'Your friend was able to clear his debts?'

'After I'd given him the money I had saved.'

'What is his name and address? It will help when he confirms what you have told us.'

The lie had already become too complicated. 'I can't answer because I haven't seen him since I gave him the money and don't know where he's living.'

'You must be worried your kind gesture doesn't turn into an unkind loss. I still need to know his name.'

'Smith. John Smith.' Unconvincing, but impossible to disprove.

'A name which we are frequently offered.'

'It's the commonest surname.'

'True, but you should not be surprised to learn I do not believe you.'

'You're conditioned to disbelieve the truth.'

'Mrs Cane is of the same opinion. Naturally, she will have phoned you to say we had questioned her over a sum of money which she drew from her husband's bank.'

It seemed there was no use in denying it. 'She cannot understand why you refused to believe her husband had given her the cheque.'

'Did she say how much that cheque was made out for?'

'No.'

'Was it for nine hundred pounds?'

'I've just said, she didn't tell me.'

'But she will have said we remarked on the coincidence that the nine hundred pounds she withdrew matched the nine hundred you paid the rent collector.'

'You're trying to suggest she gave me the money I used to pay the rent?'

'I suppose I am.'

Weariness overwhelmed him. 'You're mistaken, but I don't imagine you'll accept that's so.'

'As I have said before, I will accept what you tell me when there is reason to do so. Mr Linton, it is a criminal offence to hinder a police investigation by knowingly giving false information. You should consider the position you will be in if you continue to lie to us.'

'I have not done so.'

Bell stood. 'It seems you are unwilling to assist us in our enquiries, so there is no point in our remaining.'

As he heard them go down the stairs, Linton suffered a midnight blackness of despair. Lacking a miracle, Elaine, innocent, would soon be on trial, at the very least for having been involved in her husband's death.

Phone to his ear, Hopkins said: 'CID, Westhurst.'

'Henry here. How's the world treating you?'

'Never has and never will.'

'However mucked up I feel, a word with you makes me realize I'm quite cheerful.'

After a brief conversation, the caller said: 'We've compared the signatures in the Cane case. Fuming the cheque showed alterations were made to produce a more faithful signature.'

'Forgery?'

'As certain a ringer as you'll get without watching it being carried out.'

Hopkins reported to the detective inspector.

Bell tapped on the desk. 'We'll have Mrs Cane in. See she's asked to be here at ten, tomorrow morning.'

'I wonder if she'll have Old Foxy as her mouthpiece?'

'Probably, as he's sprung more guilty villains than there are days in the year.'

After Hopkins had left, Bell rang county HQ, was told Detective Chief Superintendent Harmsworth was at a meeting of senior officers to decide how to work for greater efficiency. Burn ninety per cent of the bloody paperwork, Bell thought as he waited to speak to Detective Superintendent Elms.

'Yes, Inspector?' Elms said.

'I have a report to make on the Cane case, sir.'

'Carry on.'

Elms was clever, smart, efficient and disliked because he judged rank to be a social distinction as well as a professional one.

'You are conversant with the details, sir?'

'Yes.'

A question he should not have thought necessary to ask. 'I have just received confirmation from Forensics that Mr Cane's signature on the cheque his wife cashed was a forgery.'

'You have asked Mr Linton to explain where the money he used to pay his overdue rent came from?'

'As to be expected, he claimed the nine hundred was what he had saved, little by little.'

'Can the claim be discounted?'

'Probably not, but I doubt the court will give it any credence.'

'Do you intend to arrest Mrs Cane?'

'I'm questioning her tomorrow and expect to do so then.'

'For murder or manslaughter?'

'Manslaughter.'

'Will the CPS accept the lesser charge?'

'They might decide there is a case for murder, sir, but I doubt that.'

'Superintendent Harmsworth will be back tomorrow, so you will report the details of the interview with Mrs Cane to him.'

Bell replaced the receiver, leaned back in the chair, stared at the wall opposite on which hung a framed photograph of the members of CID, A division, thirty-three years previously. It was no longer known if a commemorative event was being recorded, and nobody in that photo remained in service, yet it had not been removed.

Murder or manslaughter? The consequences could be similar, the difference lay in criminal responsibility. Had the victim been killed with malice aforethought? (*Mens rea*, before it had been decided to abolish pithy Latin definitions in the name of political correctness.) Had the intention been to kill or seriously injure? There was reason for Mrs Cane to have welcomed her husband's death, but had she knowingly and with malice aforethought occasioned his death? He thought not. She had seized the opportunity when, after having been assaulted by him, he had stood by the banisters at Gill Tap, too drunk to maintain his balance, and without thought she had helped him over the top rail.

'They're making me go to the police station tomorrow,' Elaine said over the phone, her voice panicky.

The official interrogation before she was charged, Linton thought.

'They've asked questions over and over again. Why are they making me go there to say the same things again?'

He lied. 'It's difficult to tell.'

'They refuse to believe me when I tell them the truth. Why? How can I make them understand? I'm so frightened.'

Innocence was a burden when others were convinced of guilt. The police believed she had had a sexual relationship with him and that they could cite facts to justify their belief. Then nothing would be lost if he now tried to still her fears. 'I'll be with you in a quarter of an hour.'

The interview room was bleakly decorated and furnished; colour and pleasant furnishings might have lessened the uneasiness of the interviewee.

'Thank you for coming here,' Bell said. As expected, a solicitor, aka 'Old Foxy', was in attendance. 'Good morning, Mr Hatch.'

Elaine was silent; Hatch returned the greeting, nodded at Morgan.

'Please sit.' He switched on the tape recorder, dictated time, place, date and those present.

'Mrs Cane, I should like you to tell me what happened on Tuesday, the twelfth of this month.'

Hatch's nickname matched his appearance and character – sharp, slinky, slippery. He said: 'You will understand, Inspector, that to do so must cause Mrs Cane great distress, especially as she has explained very precisely what did happen more than once. In view of this, perhaps you would confine yourself to any details of her past evidence which you wish to query.'

And perhaps I won't, Bell thought. 'I think it will be better to have a running statement.' He spoke to Elaine. 'You were in your bedroom when you had a sharp disagreement with your husband. What was that about?'

Earlier, in Linton's arms, she had finally explained the cause of the violent argument. He had said she must tell the police. Now, a familiar sense of shame, the thought the police would believe it had been a temporary and unusual refusal, not disgust, which had caused her to fight his demands, made her say: 'I can't remember.'

'A common failing, Mrs Cane, for both you and Mr Linton. Are you quite certain? The answer may well be in your favour, so are you certain you cannot?'

'Yes.'

'Had your husband accused you of signing a cheque in his name?'

'Mrs Cane has said she cannot remember the cause,' Hatch said.

'Did you sign a cheque in your husband's name?'

'Yes.' Linton had advised she must accept that if she were not in all likelihood to be proved a liar.

'Why did you use his signature?'

'He was not in a state to sign anything.'

'Why was it necessary for you to sign rather than wait until Mr Cane was able to do so?'

'The money was owed.' She had discussed the dilemma with Mike, and they had settled on what they thought the police would think a more plausible explanation. It shamed her to lie, but she no longer had faith that the police would believe in the truth.

'To whom?'

'Mr Linton.'

'Do you know the nature of this debt?'

'He had completed the portrait. The agreement was that he received half the fee when he finished it, half when my husband took possession of it.'

'You have a written agreement to that effect?'

'No.' It had seemed tempting fate to forge such an agreement.

'It was verbal?'

'Yes. They shook hands on it.'

'Even though your husband was a man of business and might be expected to have wanted a written contract?'

'Inspector,' Hatch said, 'there is no reason to assume a man of business will not make an agreement on the basis of trust. A handshake is a common way of sealing a deal.'

'Perhaps,' Bell answered dismissively. 'Mrs Cane, did you know Mr Linton was in debt to his landlord?'

'No.'

'On the day in question, you agree you had a heated argument with your husband. Please describe what happened then and afterwards.'

'I started to leave the bedroom. He caught me, slapped my face very hard. I managed to get free. I ran and reached the corridor when he caught me again. I fought and escaped.'

'There was no physical contact between you and him after

you broke free at the beginning of the corridor leading from the bedroom?'

'No.'

'What did you do when you left the house?'

'Drove off.'

'Did you see anyone who would confirm that?'

'I was far too upset to notice.'

'You returned to the house quite soon after leaving it. Why was that?'

'I expected John to have collapsed, as he did after drinking heavily, and I wanted to make certain he wasn't in danger of choking.'

'Even though he had physically attacked you?'

'Would you deny a wife's concern for her husband?' Hatch asked.

'After what has been described, perhaps not so many wives would show such concern. Mrs Cane, what did you discover on re-entering the house?'

'He was . . . he was . . .'

'Inspector,' Hatch said, 'Mrs Cane is in no state to continue.'

'We will adjourn for half an hour so that she may regain her composure.'

Half an hour became forty minutes before they reassembled in the interview room. The tape recorder was switched on, necessary details inputted.

'Mrs Cane, what did you find when you returned to the house, following the assault by your husband?' Bell asked.

'He lay on the floor in the hall, horribly injured.'

'After discovering this tragic fact, you phoned Mr Linton to ask for advice. Did you later that day visit him, or did he visit you?'

'No.'

'Have you been in his company since then?'

'Yes.'

'When?'

'Yesterday. He wished to express his sympathy at my husband's death.'

'He had not done so over the phone?'

'He believes commiseration should be given personally.'

'Did you not also meet him a week previously in a place known as Devil's Dyke?'

'No.'

'What is the nature of your relationship with Mr Linton?'

'Not what you seem to believe.'

'What does that mean?'

'That you think we're lovers.'

'I have never expressed such a belief.'

'You think I can't tell?'

'You mistake the import of my questions. During our enquiries, we have learned Mr Linton was painting your portrait. That has made it necessary for us to understand if he was in any way concerned with your husband's death.'

'Have you accused my client of having had an affair with Mr Linton?' Hatch asked.

'I have made no such accusation.'

'That was not my question.'

'I find it difficult to distinguish the difference.'

'Do you now accuse her of having had an affair with Mr Linton?' Hatch spoke with emphasis, as if it was necessary to speak simply and clearly.

Bell asked Elaine, 'Have you had a sexual relationship with Mr Michael Linton whilst your husband was alive?'

'No.'

'Is there anything more you wish to tell us, or any alteration you wish to make to what you have told us, concerning the events of the afternoon during which your husband tragically died?'

'I have told you exactly what happened.'

'Then, Mrs Cane, I am arresting you on a charge of manslaughter.'

In the circumstances, she had been given police bail. She sat with Linton in the Volvo on the seafront, close to where smuggled brandy had once been unloaded. The light was still good, and four miles out to sea a massive cruise ship, with the grace of a block of flats, was clearly visible as she sailed westwards.

'Mr Hatch hardly said anything!' Elaine's voice was shrill.

'He didn't argue with them, ask them why they wouldn't listen to the truth, try to defend me!'

'I'm not certain how things work,' Linton said, 'but perhaps at this stage his job was to find out as much as he could about their case and explain away any incriminating evidence.'

'How can they think I killed John? God knows, it was never a happy marriage after his illness. But even after meeting you, I tried as hard as I could to make a go of it.'

He put his arm around her and held her as close to himself as was possible in the separate front seats.

FOURTEEN

At divisional HQ, a file was prepared which included all relevant statements taken by the police from witnesses, and also statements and material unlikely to be part of the prosecution's case. This would be sent to the Director of Public Prosecutions. Because it was a case of manslaughter (perhaps to be upgraded to murder), a senior member of the service took charge of the case. It was his decision that there was insufficient evidence to warrant a charge of murder.

'No fruits, no flowers, no leaves, no birds – November.' There had been damp days, wet days, torrentially rainy days, biting winds, and the dull gloom which turned a man's thoughts to suicide or sun, sea, and sand. The last Wednesday of the month would have confounded the most fervent optimist. For Elaine and Linton, the day was the precursor to disaster.

The Honourable Sir Paul Eveley walked on to the dais, sat. In front of him, as he always demanded, was a large, new notebook, two ballpoint pens, two fountain pens charged with blue-black ink and a packet of throat pastilles. Further out of reach was a computer, which he regarded with the same dislike as a man who shot a low flying pheasant.

The court sat; the clerk of the court called the case. Elaine, in the dock, pleaded Not Guilty. Only a misogynist could not have felt sorry for her as she suffered visible despair, fear, helplessness.

Mr Justice Eveley opened the notebook and used each of the ballpoint pens to make certain it was working correctly. He checked the fountain pen was flowing. He adjusted the set of his wig. His head was an unusual shape, and the wig maker had not managed to allow for this sufficiently for the wig to remain in place if the head was sharply moved: twice during his judgeship he had had to grip it hastily to prevent its falling off and disturbing the dignity of the law; his own sense of dignity was such, he would not have suffered any embarrassment. 'Yes, Mr Jarvis.'

Jarvis stood. His instructing solicitor was on the bench in front of him, his junior on the bench behind. He had taken silk younger than most. A case concerning a celebrity, won against the odds, which would have made the headlines because of its prurient nature, would probably have seen him become famous and much requested; having lacked such a client, he was now briefed by the Crown Prosecution Service.

He addressed the bench. 'My Lord, before I begin my opening speech, I should like, with your permission, you and the jury to be handed photographs of the interior of Gill Tap, the home of Mr Cane and in which he died.'

'Very well.'

The usher handed four photographs to the judge and four to the chairman of the jury.

Jarvis studied the jury. In theory, twelve good men (or women, since the day when they had been given the right to do a man's job) and true; in this case, seven men and five women who would be swayed by the emotions and prejudices which affected all people. Already, a woman on the front row looked bored; she passed the photographs on without looking at them. A relatively young man, dressed more carefully than regretfully was often the case, was whispering to the youngish woman by his side; she smirked.

Jarvis addressed the jury in conversational style. Gone were the days when counsel used their voices and body to highlight one point, downplay another. 'Members of the jury, you are here to judge Mrs Cane on the charge of the manslaughter of her husband on the twelfth of October, in his house, Gill Tap, in the parish of Fricton.

'Manslaughter is an act of unlawful homicide which does not amount to murder. His Lordship will address you on this at a later date, but you may accept it is the act of causing the death of another without the intention of doing so, by behaving recklessly, negligently. You will ask yourselves, did the accused in any way contribute to the death of her husband? If so, was it her intention to do so?

'In this case there is clear evidence of how the victim died, but no direct evidence of why. It is my duty to explain to you how that question is to be answered.

'You will know the expression "circumstantial evidence". You may have heard it called fallible. A fact is a fact, but its interpretation is a matter of judgement and no one should claim his or her judgement to be infallible. Therefore, when presented with a fact which may point to a certain conclusion, to accept that it must is an unwarranted judgement. When there are two separate packets of information – as I will call them – which point to a conclusion, one may consider that the conclusion is *possibly* correct. If three packets point to the same conclusion, one may be tempted to accept that it *is* correct. But there cannot yet be certainty. If the packets increase in number and continue to point to the same conclusion, the necessity of doubt becomes less and less. It is the prosecution's contention that in this case, so many packets point to the same conclusion that it is the truth.'

Jarvis turned and leaned over to speak to his junior for a couple of minutes, turned back. 'Mr Cane had unfortunately suffered a ruptured blood vessel in his brain; this had the effect of altering his character. He became dissatisfied, highly critical, aggressive. It is not difficult to understand how this would alter the tempo of his and his wife's lives. The accused has admitted that her happy marriage was turned into an unhappy one, no longer placid and enjoyable.

'Mr Cane owned a security company, based in Westhurst. It was successful and was chosen to install a computer-operated security system in the premises of Aitchen and Company, who manufacture high-quality furniture and therefore maintained a large selection of valuable woods. Much of this, worth many tens of thousands of pounds, was stolen, along with valuable office and workshop equipment. In the investigation into the theft, it was discovered that one part of the security system had been faultily installed by an employee of Choopen Digital Security. It was accepted that the company would be held liable for claimed damages and this must result in the company's bankruptcy. Mr Cane requested a settlement which would avoid this result, and eventually it was agreed. Assessors for both sides decided on the amount of damages and agreed that payment would be made in two tranches, the first after the agreement was signed. In order to meet this sum, Mr Cane was forced to liquidate a large part of his capital and shut down the company. The second tranche is due before long. A careful examination of his resources shows he would be forced to sell his property and liquidate most of his remaining capital. This means he would have been without a home and with very little capital. For Mrs Cane, this presaged potential hardship. Gone would be the comfortable life, in material terms, which she had been leading. Gone would be the historical home. There would be little possibility of holidays abroad. Housekeeping would be on a restricted budget.

'Mrs Cane must have faced the future with despair. Nothing is more emotionally depressing than to lose the standard of living one has enjoyed. Then she remembered her husband held a life assurance for three quarters of a million pounds. The premium was considerable, and it was possible he would no longer be able to meet it, yet should he die in an accident before the next premium was due, the assured sum would be hers. A proportion would have to be paid to Aitchen and Company to meet the second tranche of the settlement, but what remained would enable her to keep her home and would ensure her lifestyle remained reasonably pleasant.

'You will hear that some time before his death, Mr Cane had asked Mr Linton to paint a portrait of his wife. Does that seem reasonable when Mr Cane was facing grave financial problems? Might it be that his wife beguiled him into this very rash expenditure because the painter was someone for whom she had developed a regard? She will say she had not met Mr Linton before the party at which her husband made that request. You will decide whether, under normal circumstances, a man would commission a portrait of his wife which he could not afford.

'Both Mrs Cane and Mr Linton will quote the amount that

was to be paid on completion of the portrait and on Mr Cane's taking possession of it, yet neither can produce a signed contract with the terms recorded. Mr Linton – a specialist in nude paintings – will probably not claim to be a noted or even well-known artist, so why should he have been chosen? That is unless, perhaps, he agreed to paint the portrait for considerably less than, as you will hear, is now claimed.

'Mrs Cane's portrait was painted in Mr Linton's studio. This is the upper floor of a disused mill and offers very few facilities. It contains a bed – referred to as a prop – two chairs, a makeshift changing room, a WC and odd pieces of furniture. Not, one would think, a place in which one would wish to spend any more time than was essential. You may well ask yourselves why was the portrait painted there and not in Mrs Cane's home where she would have been very much more comfortable and at ease. It is difficult to believe Mr Linton could genuinely have found good reason to object. As a snail carries his home around with it, an artist can carry the necessities of his work to where he wishes.

'The studio did offer one advantage: the absence of Mr Cane. It is the prosecution's case that Mrs Cane and Mr Linton entered into a relationship which went far beyond that of painter and sitter. A relationship with many precedents in the art world.

'You will see and hear Mr Linton in the witness-box. You will make your own judgements and may well believe that when Mrs Cane, emotionally disturbed because of the present nature of her marriage, went to the studio and was with a man only a year or two older than herself and noticeably younger than her husband, a man who was good looking, sympathetic and – at least in her own mind – endowed with the carefree, fun-seeking character of the traditional painter, she was attracted to him. The prosecution says that the degree of this attraction plays a vital part in the case.

'Mrs Cane has repeatedly denied she has enjoyed a relationship with Mr Linton other than that which arose from painter and subject. Yet you will learn there was a constant stream of telephone calls between them, far exceeding any reasonable explanation for the need of painter and subject to converse.

'On the day Mr Cane died, Mrs Cane, having learned of his violent death, phoned Mr Linton. Some nine minutes later, she called for a doctor, after speaking to Mr Linton to ask him what to do. You may well consider that one would normally call a doctor to report a death before asking for personal advice. And why should she seek that advice from someone with whom, in her own words, she had a friendly relationship simply because he was painting her? The prosecution will say that during Mr Cane's lifetime, Mr Linton and Mrs Cane enjoyed an adulterous relationship.

'Shortly after Mr Cane's death, Mr Linton was called upon to pay the overdue rent for the lease of his studio or he would be thrown out of his tenancy. The sum involved was nine hundred pounds. Despite an admitted lack of success and therefore finances, Mr Linton paid the due sum. Before this, Mrs Linton signed a cheque in her husband's name and cashed it at her husband's bank. It was for nine hundred pounds.

'On the day of Mr Cane's death, he and his wife had a bitter row, involving physical violence on both their parts. When asked what caused this row, Mrs Cane denied she could remember, claiming that events had bewildered her. Can you, members of the jury, believe that a wife, having been attacked by her husband, can not remember the reason for his attack? Is it not likely that Mr Cane had learned his wife had drawn nine hundred pounds out of his bank and had demanded to know why? And that when she refused to answer, he decided that his suspicions were correct and she had given the money to her lover?

'Mrs Cane says that she escaped from the bedroom, but her husband caught her in the short passage leading to the balcony and she struggled violently before she managed to break free. During the struggle, a small portion of her dress, on which was a button, was torn free. By her evidence, this fell just outside the bedroom. Yet it was found by the banisters on the balcony.

'During the investigation into Mr Cane's death, a careful examination of the banisters was made in order to judge whether a man of his height and build, standing against the banisters, would be in danger of falling over them if he failed to maintain his balance. You will hear that this was unlikely; that in all probability there would need to be added momentum to cause him to go over them rather than collapse against them.

'A wife, verbally and physically abused by her husband, is

accused by him of signing his name on a cheque in order to draw nine hundred pounds to give to her lover. Enraged by her denials, he grasps her. She breaks free, escapes from the bedroom, runs in to the passage and out on to the balcony. He catches her. There is a fierce struggle in which a piece of her dress and a button are torn off. In the course of the struggle, he comes up against the top rail of the banisters. Were no force applied to his upper body, he would be unlikely to fall over them. Yet he fell.

'Why did he fall? That is the question you have to ask your-selves. Did the accused accidentally gain sufficient adverse momentum to cause him to overcome the security provided by the height of the banisters? Then it was an accidental death and the accused is guilty of no offence. Or did she become aware of the potentially dangerous situation in which he was? Did the humiliation she had suffered, did the thought that were he dead, she would be free openly to live with her lover, encourage her to apply the pressure which changed accidental death to unlawful homicide? Is a sense of guilt responsible for her alleged loss of memory, or the many lies she has given? It is you, members of the jury, who will decide.' Jarvis sat.

Logan, Jarvis' junior, questioned Doctor Waldron, since he could be expected to give undisputed evidence.

'You were called to Gill Tap on Tuesday, the twelfth of October?'

'That is correct.'

'Will you tell the court what you found?'

'Lying on the floor in the hall was a man who had suffered violent trauma to his head. I confirmed he was dead, then I escorted Mrs Cane to her bedroom and attended to her.'

'In what state did you find her?'

'Extremely shocked and hysterical. I decided it was necessary to administer a sedative.'

'Did Mrs Cane say anything which could explain what had happened?'

'No; she made no comment.'

'Did anything about her appearance attract your attention?'

'There was severe bruising on her right cheek. Under the nails of two of the fingers of her right hand was an alien substance.'

'Could you judge what that was?'

'I thought it was probably human skin.'

'What did you do next?'

'Returned downstairs and examined the body of the deceased.'

'What did your examination reveal?'

'There were two fairly deep scratches on the left side of the neck and bruising on his chest.'

'Did you come to any conclusion as to how these injuries had been sustained?'

'It seemed likely there had been physical violence between husband and wife. I informed the police that they should investigate the circumstances.'

The cross-examination was perfunctory.

The forensic pathologist said: 'I examined the nails of Mrs Cane's hands. There was little of note under the nails of the left hand, but I took a sample. Behind the nails of two of the fingers on her right hand, however, was a substance I suspected was blood and skin. I used a spatula to remove this, and again I put it into a bottle which was given to a police constable.'

He was handed two small, plastic exhibit bottles.

'Do you identify the handwriting on the bottles?'

'It is mine.'

'Are the contents that which you scraped from under Mrs Cane's nails?'

'They are.'

'What are they?'

'One bottle contains little of note. That is the bottle containing scrapings from the left nails. The other bottle, containing scrapings from the right nails, holds human blood and skin.'

'Were you able to identify from whom it had come?'

'Tests showed it to have been torn out of the dead man's neck.'

'Did you examine the bruises on the deceased's chest?'

'I did.'

'Were you able to reach a conclusion as to how they had been caused?'

'In my opinion, they were from the blows of a fist or fists. Their nature suggested the person concerned possessed no great strength.'

Cross-examination was brief.

'Is there any way in which the actual force of a blow on skin can be measured?'

'It can only be judged by the nature of the bruise or damage to flesh and bone.'

'A man using only part of his strength may well inflict a bruise no greater than that which a woman might cause?'

'In my experience, blows are delivered with the maximum force the assailant can provide.'

Quinn remembered the old adage: when cross-examining, never ask that one question too many.

It was a typical suburban restaurant: a place where one ate not for the pleasure, but to satisfy hunger. Linton had no regard to the food as his mind suffered bitter guilt. If he had not mentioned the threat of eviction to Elaine, had not agreed to meet her at Devil's Dyke, above all had not fallen in love with her, she would not now be on trial.

He ate a portion of sherry trifle without recording its blandness. The case was going badly. Prosecution's opening speech, calmly given, had woven a cloak of guilt. Could defence counsel tear it apart? So far, he had offered no suggestion he might.

He finished his meal, left the restaurant. A light drizzle drifted down from the grey sky. His sense of fear and self blame increased as he neared the Crown Court.

Witnesses were called, their evidence guiding the court through the police investigation – the call summoning the police, the degree of Cane's intoxication, the torn-off piece of Elaine's dress on the balcony, the search for the brown Volkswagen Beetle, the identification of Linton, the sighting of him and the occupant of a white Volvo in an amorous embrace at Devil's Dyke . . .

FIFTEEN

Jarvis looked down at a page of his brief, briefly read, looked up. 'Mr Tamworth, you are a solicitor, a partner in the firm of Tamworth and Shuttleleave, whose registered address is in Westhurst?'

'That is correct.' His narrow face, which ended with a jutting-out chin, made him a prime subject for a cartoonist.

'Are you responsible for the legal affairs of Choopen Digital Security?'

'I was consulted by the firm when they deemed this necessary.'

'Were you consulted after Aitchen and Company laid a claim against Choopen Digital Security when they had suffered a burglary which resulted in valuable timber and equipment being stolen?'

'I was.'

'What were the consequences to Choopen of this theft?'

'A mistake in the installation of the security system was found to be due to the negligence of one of their employees. This resulted in a claim for damages against the company which was likely to be successful. In order to avoid a court case and the very considerable cost to both sides this would entail, an agreement was finally reached between the company and Mr Cane. He would pay the agreed amount: half on signature, half in six months.'

'Was the first half paid on time?'

'Yes.'

'Can you say by what means?'

'By the sale of the company, boosted by a capital input from Mr Cane.'

'Did you know how he proposed paying the final amount?'

'I am not aware of the exact details.'

'As far as you could know, was he likely to be left in reduced circumstances?'

'It seemed very probable.'

'Was his wife aware of that fact?'

'I have no idea.'

'Thank you.'

Quinn stood. He was six foot three, broad shoulders, an amateur rugby player of some note. He had been given a red bag by a silk with whom he had appeared fairly early in his career; confirmation that, as Elaine had been assured, he was sharp (despite asking that one question too many). 'Mr Tamworth, did Mr Cane ever tell you, either directly or indirectly, that he had discussed the financial problems of his firm with his wife?'

'No.'

'You have reason to think he might have done?'

'No. On the contrary, he once told me that a good businessman never discussed his work with a woman.'

'Thank you.'

Tamworth left the witness-box.

Carter-Johnson took the oath and gave identification evidence.

'You are an assistant bank manager?' Jarvis asked.

'Yes,' Carter-Johnson agreed.

'Did Mr Cane have an account at your branch?'

'He had two. One in the name of the company, to which his manager also had access; the other was his private account, which was reserved to himself.'

'It was not a joint account with his wife?'

'As I have just tried to make clear.'

'At the time of his death, what was the amount in each account?'

'The company account had been temporarily frozen. His private one was in debit far beyond the agreed limit of overdraft.'

'Had he been asked to reduce the overdraft?'

'Yes.'

'Had he done so?'

'No.'

'Did you take steps to encourage repayment?'

'I asked him to come to my office. When he did so, I told him I regretted having to explain the consequences of his not clearing the overdraft.'

'How did he respond?'

'He expressed the probability of his being able to do so in the near future.'

'Did he explain how that might be?'

'He seemed to be relying on the not unusual mixture of hope and optimism. However, taking into account his previous excellent financial position, I agreed to renew his overdraft for a further six months if he would, in turn, agree to pay off a set amount each month.'

'Did he manage a reduction after speaking to you?'

'No; the contrary. He became further overdrawn.'

'Did you take any steps to enforce repayment?'

'His death made any such immediate action irresponsible.'

Jarvis sat.

Quinn stood. It had been remarked that opposing barristers in court evoked memories of the weather-forecasting model with a wet or dry figure emerging from a house. 'How was Mr Cane's credit worthiness rated before the claim of negligence against his company?'

'A1.'

'Thank you.'

Mrs Owen was called. She entered the courtroom unawed, regarded the bewigged judge and counsel with condescending interest. She took the oath; because her dentures were not fitting as well as they had been, she ended by appearing to say 'so swelp me God'.

'You are Mrs Margaret Owen and you live at thirty-seven St. Arlott Street, East Fricton?'

'Yes.'

'You work at Gill Tap?'

'Yes.'

'Roughly for how long have you done so?'

'Nigh on three years.'

'During that time, have you frequently met and spoken to Mr and Mrs Cane?'

'It was her. Most of the time, he was at work.'

'Did you have reason to judge the nature of their relationship?'

'She wore a ring. They was man and wife.'

'I will rephrase the question. Do you think they were a happy couple who got on very well together?'

'He didn't make it happy for her.'

'In what way did he not do so?'

'Drinking and going on at her all the time.'

'They often had disagreements?'

'If my Bert ever spoke to me as he often did to her, I'd of given him an earful. I told her that.'

'How did Mrs Cane respond to your comment?'

'Said it was the fault of the illness he'd had.'

'Did you ever have reason to believe Mr Cane struck his wife?'

'No.'

'Did you ever hear him threaten her?'

'Heard him call her a block of ice and he'd bloody well melt her.'

'How did she respond?'

'Never said anything.'

Quinn flicked the tails of his wig away from his neck as he stood and began his cross-examination. 'Mrs Cane told you her husband's attitude was a result of the illness which he suffered some years previously. Then you think she bore little resentment because of his behaviour?'

'She was too good for him.'

'What makes you say that?'

'Never shouted back, didn't matter what he said. Didn't have a go at him for his drinking.'

'Would you think she still had affection for him?'

'Of course she did.'

'Despite his behaviour?'

'You don't understand the kind of person she is.'

'What kind is she?'

'Being married to him, she looked after him, however bad he treated her.'

Quinn hesitated. Continue the cross-examination to impress on the jury that Elaine had shown only care and affection for her husband, however he treated her? Remember that last question. 'Thank you.'

Jarvis re-examined. 'Mrs Owen, you seem to judge the Cane's marriage was not a happy one.'

'Not being deaf, it weren't difficult to know that.'

'One can mistake the import of what one hears.'

'What's that supposed to mean?'

'One may hear something and, through one reason or another, mistake joshing for rudeness.'

'If someone calls me a stupid bitch, I ain't so stupid as to think he's joshing.'

'Did you hear Mr Cane call Mrs Cane a stupid bitch?'

'More than once.'

'Do you know the reason for his doing so?'

'He didn't ever need no reason to swear at her.'

'Was he friendly to you?'

'Him! He'd no time for the likes of me.'

Jarvis was satisfied the jury would understand her evidence was very biased. He sat, leaving his junior to continue the immediate case in the knowledge that the information given would be of little consequence.

Quinn began his opening address. 'This case contains features which demand the greatest attention on your part. The prosecution's case lacks hard evidence and relies too heavily on circumstantial evidence. My learned friend gave you a precise explanation of the form, manner and consequences of this. His Lordship will no doubt comment at depth on this in his summing-up. What I want to do now is show how, when it forms the major part of a case, circumstantial evidence can appear to bear such force it can no longer be challenged. You have to remember that it *must* be challenged, and interpretations must be weighed for possible mistakes.

'What is hard evidence? It is evidence that cannot be refuted or explained away, that is not open to any possibility other than that which is asserted. What is circumstantial evidence? If I see A with a gun in his hand shoot B in broad daylight, my sight unhindered, that is hard evidence. If I see A holding a gun enter a building, hear a shot, he returns and runs away, at that moment there is only circumstantial evidence to hold he fired the shot which killed B.

'For circumstantial evidence to be accepted requires supporting evidence. To return to A and B. A admits he did have a gun in his hand, did go into the building, meet B and had a bit of a tussle. B gained hold of the gun and accidentally discharged it while the muzzle was pointing at himself. An apparent accident. But if it is shown A and B were known to dislike each other, that very recently they had had an argument during which A uttered threats, that A stood to gain in some way by B's death – these are reasons to judge that A knowingly, and with malice aforethought, killed B. It is up to a jury to decide if the circumstances are sufficiently valid to convince them A is a liar.

'Mrs Cane is charged with the manslaughter of her husband. In long past years, such a charge would result, if she were found guilty, in her death by extreme measures. As Talist wrote: "Even Zeus flinches when a man is evilly smitten by his wife." Evil is corruption of the soul. When you look at the accused, can you see corruption of soul? Of course not. You see a woman, incapable of so heinous an evil, brought before you, suffering the stress of innocence.

'The prosecution claims many facts and incidents are linked together. Yet study each one very closely and you will understand that not one points to my client's guilt. Mr Cane decided he wanted a portrait of his wife painted and was advised to commission Mr Linton. Mr Linton is a professional painter who, after some years, has yet to meet great success. This is a common occurrence. Some would say it is *obligatory* in the art world. He met Mr and Mrs Cane for the first time at a cocktail party. Due to illness, Mr Cane had suffered a change of character and unfortunately his marriage had become an unhappy one.

'These are facts. The prosecution suggests that Mrs Cane encouraged her husband to commission Mr Linton because of a previous deep friendship between herself and Mr Linton. This is denied by both parties. It is to put the cart before the horse. Avoid that mistake.

'The prosecution has made much of the fact that after a serious row with her husband, Mrs Cane says she broke free from his second assault when just inside the passage between the bedroom and the balcony. A button on a small piece of her frock was found near the banisters on the balcony. The prosecution claims this proves the second struggle took place by the banisters, not just outside the bedroom as Mrs Cane claims, and in the course of it she helped him over the banisters. That is to decide on the conclusion and interpret the facts to meet this; to ignore the possibilities and probabilities.

'Is there a shred of evidence to deny the probability that the piece of dress and button had been torn loose during the course of the argument, but had not fallen off her until, desperately racing to avoid him, turning to get down the stairs, they finally fell by the banisters?'

Quinn spoke for another twenty minutes.

Linton gave his evidence for the defence. When Jarvis stood to begin his cross-examination, Linton knew pure hatred for the man who was trying to prove Elaine guilty.

'You are by profession an artist?'

'I am.'

'Are you successful?'

'If I knew how to define success, I might think I was to some extent.' A defensive answer, unlikely to defend.

'Are you an elected academician?'

'No.'

'Do you submit your works at the summer exhibition at the Royal Academy?'

'Sometimes.'

'Have many of your works have been accepted?'

'My style of painting is currently out of fashion.'

'You are admitting none of your paintings has been accepted?'

A pause.

'Are you with any art dealer in London?'

'No.'

'In one of the major provincial cities?'

'No.'

'Do you paint commercially – by which I mean work to a set requirement for an agreed fee?'

'I paint pictures for a magazine.'

'The name of the magazine?'

Jarvis was the cat; he was the mouse to be played with until the kill. '*Macho Miscellany.*'

'It has the sound of a magazine for men. Is that so?'

'Women are free to buy it.'

'Let us find out if they are likely to. What subjects do you paint for *Macho Miscellany*?'

'Young women.'

'Fashion paintings?'

'Naked,' he said curtly, to deprive prosecuting counsel of further sneering, sarcastic conjectures.

'Which, of course, is a favourite subject of artists over the centuries. Do you paint them in any particular style?'

'In no particular style.'

'Might they be described as semi-pornographic?'

'People found classical Victorian paintings pornographic that today could never be thought of as such. Pornography cannot be defined.'

'Perhaps not in an artist's mind, but it certainly can be in an intelligent person's mind. Was Mrs Cane aware of the nature of these paintings?'

'She knew I had to make a living.'

'You are saying that she was aware?'

'Up to a point.'

'What point?'

'I mentioned what I was doing.'

'Did you show her a copy of the magazine?'

'No.'

'Did you explain that the naked young ladies were asked to pose in a certain fashion?'

'No.'

'Perhaps your lack of detail was because Mrs Cane would have been somewhat shocked by your work. Is it not, therefore, remarkable for her to have recommended your work to her husband?'

'She did not recommend me.'

'You have been painting a portrait of Mrs Cane?'

'Yes.'

'Clothed, I believe. You have told the court a friend introduced you at a cocktail party. How long after this were you commissioned to paint the portrait?'

'It was at the party itself.'

'Mrs Cane was at the party when her husband made this request. Was it not she who suggested it?'

'As I said, he had been told by a friend that I was a proficient artist.'

'You discussed the details of the commission with Mr Cane the next day, but the details were not agreed immediately?'

'He had been called to his office.'

'Was Mrs Cane present?'

'She said her husband would probably not be long and suggested I remained.'

'When did Mr Cane return?'

'Not until the early afternoon.'

'By which time, of course, you had left?'

'No. When her husband did not show up as expected, Mrs Cane said I should stay and have lunch with her.'

'Her offer must have surprised you?'

'Why should it have done? I accepted it as a kind gesture, from a kind person, as a small recompense for a wasted morning.'

'You were able to judge her motive on so short an acquaintance?'

'An artist learns to understand a sitter's character, and character provides motive.'

'When Mr Cane returned, the commission was confirmed. What was to be your fee?'

'Eighteen hundred pounds.'

'To be paid in two tranches. Did Mr Cane not suggest a contract, and did you not deny that was necessary?'

'No.'

'It is unusual for a businessman to enter a verbal contract with someone he barely knows.'

'It is unusual for a businessman to have any contact with art.'

'You say he did not suggest you paint his wife at his home?'

'As I have already explained, I prefer to work in my studio because I find it easier to attune to what I'm doing.'

'The painting is finished, and you say you have been paid the first tranche. How many sittings did Mrs Cane give you?'

'I don't know the number.'

'Few or many?'

'Quite a few.'

'The two of you were on your own on many occasions?'

'And I spent that time painting.'

'There is a reason for your saying what to most would seem obvious?'

'You were trying to insinuate something,' Linton said angrily.

'I was merely remarking that there were many occasions on which you were able to discern her nature, as you have told us is an artist's task. However, since you have raised the possibility, did these frequent meetings, in private, not create an affectionate relationship?'

'A friendship.'

'Nothing more?'

'Mrs Cane was married.'

'Hardly a hindrance to adulterous relationships these days.'

'She would never commit adultery.'

'How can you so confidently assert that?'

'Because of her character.'

'How would you describe your present relationship with Mrs Cane?'

'As I have said, we are friends.'

'You and Mrs Cane often converse with each other when she is not in your studio, being painted?'

'We talk over the telephone.'

'You must have a great deal to discuss, remembering the number of calls between you. You have said Mrs Cane phoned you on Tuesday, the twelfth of October?'

'Yes.'

'It was the day her husband died, and she asked you for your advice as to what to do. Did you not wonder why she phoned you, a friend, but by your own description not a close one, for advice? When one needs help, one usually calls on someone there is every reason to believe will give it.'

'When in a panic, as Mrs Cane naturally was, one does not think logically. She is a lady without much family, so she must have been at a loss who to call on for aid.'

'You twice phoned Gill Tap to ask how Mrs Cane was. The

PC on duty described you as having been extremely concerned about Mrs Cane.'

'Naturally, knowing what had happened.'

'We have heard that some time after those calls, you drove to Gill Tap and spoke to the duty PC. She gained the impression you were aware that Mr Cane was confirmed dead.'

'She was mistaken; I only knew what Mrs Cane, in her distress, had told me.'

'Did you like Mr Cane?'

'I saw so little of him, I neither liked nor disliked him.'

'The police constable reported you appeared so emotionally concerned about Mrs Cane's condition, your relationship with her must be more than mere friendship.'

'She was talking nonsense. How could she gain any such impression without knowing me?'

'Police men and women are trained to judge a person by his or her manner, speech, and body language. Something which, as you have assured us, you also do in your profession. Are you in love with Mrs Cane?'

'What do you mean by the question?'

'It is not obvious?'

'I have never committed adultery with her.'

'You are very eager to deny sexual activity, even though it has not been alleged. One might think such unnecessary denial indicative.'

'One might think a Snark is a Boojum.'

'You own an ancient and rather worn Volkswagen Beetle. Mrs Cane owns a white Volvo estate car. Such two cars were seen on the rock shelf in the Devil's Dyke, and the two occupants were seen to embrace with much vigour. You were asked by the police if the two persons concerned were Mrs Cane and you, and you denied that they were. Yet you refused to name the lady you say you were with. Why?'

'I was not going to have her mixed up in this.'

'The police would have ensured her name was not made public.'

'No one can ensure anonymity these days.'

'By refusing to name her, you must increase the suspicion she was Mrs Cane.'

'*I* know it was not she.'

'Chivalry before truth?'

The judge said: 'An unnecessary remark, Mr Jarvis.'

'I withdraw it, My Lord.' He turned and spoke to Logan sotto voce. 'Pompous old bastard. I thought it was rather apt.' He faced the witness-box again. 'You had recently failed to pay the rent due on the studio. Three months were owing. The rent collector arrived when two detectives were present, and they heard him demand the overdue amount – nine hundred pounds. Your explanation for not having paid the rent when due is that you had lent money to a friend named "John Smith" whose current whereabouts you are ignorant of. That is correct?'

'Yes.'

'Yet you were able to pay the rent collector nine hundred pounds. How was this?'

'Mrs Cane had paid me the first instalment for the portrait.'

'Yet when first interviewed by the police, you suggested you had merely saved up for the rent, little by little.'

'I had forgotten about the payment.'

'A regrettable lapse of memory!'

Linton said nothing.

'Prior to your settlement of the rent, Mrs Cane withdrew nine hundred pounds from her husband's account on a cheque signed by her using her husband's name. By a remarkable coincidence, the amount of rent due was also nine hundred pounds. Do you still wish to claim that the payment was for the portrait?'

'Yes. The similar amounts are, as you say, a coincidence.'

'The arm of coincidence seems to have grown beyond an arm's length. Had you not mentioned to Mrs Cane that you were in fear of eviction?'

'No.'

'Had you done so, being a woman with the nature you tell us she has, she would have wanted to help you, wouldn't she?'

'I did not tell her.'

The cross-examination continued.

Re-examination was brief.

Linton watched Elaine leave the dock and descend out of sight, followed by a PC. When she had looked at him at the last moment, her despair had equalled his.

He was one of the last to leave the courtroom, yet in the hall there were still a number of people. A PC spoke to a man in overalls. 'What are you doing here, George?'

'Trouble with the electricity. What about you?'

'Court duties.'

'A day off work, then. What's going on?'

'A wife's up for knocking off her husband.'

Linton, about to pass, came to a halt.

'New kind of women's lib?'

'He was worth more dead than alive.'

'D'you reckon she did it?'

'They'll be getting her cell ready.'

Linton wanted to shout she was innocent, innocent! He walked on. His mind foretold the future. What is your verdict? Guilty. Prisoner, you are condemned to life imprisonment. Van with blackened windows, prison gates, an order to strip, invasive body search, a cell shared with a prostitute, harshly expressed contempt from fellow inmates because she was not of their background . . .

He ran out of the hall to escape its malign influence.

He sat on the bed in his studio, his bitter mind unable to leave the past. Her portrait was over there to remind him how they had talked without constraint, fallen in love; he was sitting on the bed on which their desires had been stilled because of her loyalty to her concept of marriage . . .

A woman called out from below. 'Are you there, Mike?'

He recognized Betty's voice and did not answer, hoping she would leave. He heard her climb the wooden stairs as her high heels resounded on the boards. She came into the studio, dressed in a manner that followed fashion at the cost of comfort.

'I knew you were here because the door was unlocked.' She came to a halt in front of the bed. 'You haven't been in touch.'

'I've been tied up.'

She hesitated, spoke quickly. 'Mike, speak it straight. Don't you want me to work for you any more?' Worry creased her face. She depended on his money as much as he depended on that from the magazine.

'I want you back as soon as feasible.'

'I don't understand.'

'Until the trial's over, I can't do any work.'

'Are you being had up for something?'

'Haven't you read about it?'

'I don't know what you're talking about. What's happened?'

'Someone I know is on trial and in terrible trouble. I've been called as a witness and turned inside out by a clever bastard of a lawyer. It must be in the papers and on the telly, surely?'

'Who's the someone?'

'Elaine Cane.'

'It's her?' She pointed at the portrait.

'Yes.'

'There's been nothing about you or her in the news.'

He had assumed that because the trial was of such bitter importance to him, it would have been of prurient interest to others. The egotism of the sufferer. 'Betty, did the police question you about the painting?'

'Why should they have?'

'Elaine is charged with killing her husband. The law thinks we were in love, that she killed him in order to claim his life insurance money and be with me. If you'd told them you were certain I was in love with the subject of the portrait, it would have strengthened their case.'

'Do you believe she could have done it?'

'Goddamnit, you're like them and think she did?'

'I don't know anything, Mike. Can't you tell them she'd never do such a terrible thing?'

'I tried and bloody failed.'

She reached across and briefly put her hands on his. 'Is it very tough for you?'

'I've done everything possible, but might as well have just waited to see her sent to jail for God knows how long.'

'Mike . . .'

He looked at her.

'Mike, you're in a terrible state. Would it help if you screwed me?'

To have sex with her might bring a certain relief, however temporary. Yet he knew that later he would consider it had, in a sense, degraded his love for Elaine. Betty would not understand that. She was trying to help him by offering what she could. 'No one could ever be kinder than you've just been, Betty. But I'm emotionally in rags and would be like a pricked balloon.'

'When the balloon blows up again, phone.' She stood, leaned over and kissed him on the cheek. 'I don't believe there's anyone to listen, but I'll still be praying for you and her.'

She crossed to the door. 'If only you were like Terry. But you ain't.' She left.

SIXTEEN

Jarvis' manner remained courteous. An experienced thief who had been questioned by him in court had once remarked: 'The old bugger was so pleasant, I nearly told the truth.'

'Mrs Cane, we have heard that on the twelfth of October, your husband was inebriated early in the day. Did this often happen?'

'He usually started drinking later in the day,' she answered.

'Do you know why he drank heavily?'

'It was probably from frustration. Illness had left him not as mentally clear or level-headed as he had been.'

'Might not his frustration have been due to circumstances in your marriage?'

'No!'

The sharpness of her answer satisfied Jarvis that, as he had implied and hoped the jury would accept, frustration had resulted from sexual reluctance caused by her love for Linton. 'There was a fierce argument between the two of you on that Tuesday. What was the argument about?'

'I can't remember.'

'Nevertheless, will you give the jury a brief résumé of the content.'

'I said, I can't remember!'

'Can't, Mrs Cane, or won't? Was it over something you had done?'

'Why won't you understand? He was drunk, and he attacked me. I was terrified! It was a nightmare. I remember when he hit me, but after that, it's like a fog.'

'But not so foggy that you have forgotten you ran and he caught you, that in an effort to break free, you raked his neck with your nails, even though he was not in command of himself and could not have intended to hurt you.'

'If you were attacked, would you worry whether or not it was intentional?'

He was surprised she should suddenly show a spirit of resistance. 'You broke free and reached the passage, where he caught you a second time. With memory restored, you say that is where he tore off the piece of your frock with a button on it?'

'It must have been.'

'Unless he caught you a third time by the banisters.'

'He didn't.'

'I suggest, Mrs Cane, that knowing the button was found by the banisters on the balcony, it was clear to you that the only way of avoiding the conclusion that that was where he tore the dress, you had to lie about the sequence of events. I put it to you that you raced away from the bedroom but, being a faster runner, your husband caught you by the banisters and it was there that the piece of dress was torn free.

'We have heard evidence that a man of Mr Cane's height and build, standing against them, is only just in balance – by which I mean that the top rail is below his centre of gravity, so additional momentum is likely to topple him over them, to fall to the floor below. When you broke free, was he not against the banisters, unsteady because of his drunkenness and therefore in considerable danger? Did you not, in response to his assaults and your emotions, unbalance him sufficiently to send him over the banisters?'

'He was still on the balcony when I ran out of the house,' she said wildly.

'Before you left, you claim you turned round and saw him there. Yet if you were fleeing from him, would you not have expected him to be pursuing you down into the hall? Any hesitation on your part, under such circumstances, would have been fatal, as he would have caught you.'

'He was shouting and swearing from the balcony.'

'You had no need for further panic, then?'

'I wasn't aware of anything but the need to escape the house.'

'You have given evidence to the police and in this court, yet this is the first time you have mentioned his shouting at you from the balcony as you left the house. I put it to you that this is a lie, an attempt to persuade the court your husband was alive as you left when in fact you knew he lay on the floor of the hall, fatally injured.'

'He *was* still alive!' she said wildly.

'You say that after leaving the house, you drove around to try to overcome what had happened. Where did you go?'

'I don't remember.'

'Your memory appears to have been in such a state of shock, it was inadvisable for you to drive anywhere. For how long did you drive?'

'I don't know.'

'For ten minutes, twenty minutes?'

'I can't tell you.'

'Further to this, you say you parked the car and sat for a while. Where did you park your car, Mrs Cane?'

'I can't remember.'

'How long for?'

'I said, I can't remember!'

'Very well, Mrs Cane. I will leave the jury to draw their own conclusions. What persuaded you to return?'

'I've explained.'

'I would like you to do so again.'

'Sometimes John is . . . was . . .'

'Yes?'

'Sick. I was afraid he might choke.'

'You would like the jury to accept that, terrified, having had to fight free of him to escape, you then returned to make certain he was all right?'

'Yes.'

'Very well. On your return, you found your husband lying on the floor of the hall, having suffered severe injuries. You phoned Mr Linton for help. Why?'

'I didn't know what to do.'

'You thought it more likely he could help than the emergency services, who would be able to take steps to save his life if he were not dead?'

She clenched the edge of the dock with whitening fingers.

'Did you call Mr Linton immediately on your return, or did a period of time elapse between your return and the call?'

'I . . . I checked to see if John was breathing. He was . . . he was . . . was cold to the touch. I can't remember if I called right away. You must understand! It was *terrible!*'

Jarvis waited for her to recover her composure, decided he could not continue this course of cross-examination unless he wished to appear heartless, which would not help his case. 'At the time of your marriage, was the difference in age between you and your husband twenty-four years?'

'Yes.'

'What was your occupation when you met him?'

'I was a secretary.'

'You were not highly paid?'

'I received an average wage.'

'Was Mr Cane living in Gill Tap?'

'Yes.'

'Did you know he owned Choopen Digital Security?'

'Yes.'

'Did you have reason to think it was a successful company?'

'Yes.'

'Then, before your marriage, he was considerably older than you, but was enjoying the material benefits of success?'

'If you're trying to say—' She stopped abruptly.

'I am merely establishing facts, Mrs Cane.'

'I married him because I loved him.'

'Your marriage, we have heard, was initially happy. But ceased to be so when Mr Cane very unfortunately suffered an illness which changed his character and he became argumentative and aggressive.'

'He couldn't help that.'

'To have a warm and, you assure us, loving marriage suddenly become one of discord, inevitably must cause stress and sorrow. How did you deal with this?'

'I had to, so I did.'

'Did you seek the help of friends?'

'We had few friends by then.'

'Family?'

'I am an only child, and my parents died some years ago.'

'You became lonely?'

'I have always been self-sufficient.'

'Yet a relatively young woman, married to an older man who through misfortune has caused the marriage to become unhappy, must welcome meeting someone of roughly her own age who is amusing and friendly. Would you not agree?'

'It's possible.'

'And it is likely that that friend will become a very firm and valued friend?'

She gave no answer.

'Will you explain, in greater detail than you provided when questioned by my learned friend, how you came to meet Mr Linton.'

Even in her distressed, confused state, she understood he was raising in the minds of the jury an image of a young, poorly paid woman chasing an older man who, in her eyes, was wealthy; of her discontent at the reality of that marriage, wishing for life to hold more fun and excitement, and meeting a man of her own age who could offer her that. 'It's not how you think it is,' she said wildly.

'Mrs Cane, what I think is of no account. What I seek are the facts. Will you please tell the court how you came to meet Mr Linton?'

She turned to look at Linton, seeking the help he was desperate to give her, yet could not.

'You would rather not answer?'

'We were asked to a cocktail party. He was there.'

'You got into conversation, as one does at such parties?'

'He was introduced to us as a talented painter.'

'You have said you do not know who named him as such?'

'I don't.'

'It was not you, hoping your husband would engage him to paint your portrait?'

'No. I've said again and again, it *wasn't*!'

'Since then, have you seen any paintings, other than your portrait, by Mr Linton?'

'No.'

'But you were aware that they were far removed from that work?'

'He said they were purely commercial.'

'They are paintings of naked women in postures many would regard as risqué and some would term pornographic.'

'He said that until one became well known, one had to paint whatever was wanted.'

'It is very unlikely he would show such paintings to someone in order to gain the commission for a portrait, so one has to wonder how your "someone" came to advise your husband that he was so good a painter, he should do your portrait. I again put it to you that it was *you* who advised your husband to ask Mr Linton to paint your portrait.'

'I keep saying it wasn't. Why won't you believe me?'

'Because, to paraphrase inexpertly, the truth isn't what you choose it to mean. You told the police you were not aware your husband had a life assurance for three quarters of a million pounds; you have told my learned friend you did not know this. Is that true?'

'I keep telling the truth, but you won't believe me!'

'Your husband did not mention the fact before or after your marriage?'

'No.'

'One must expect him to have eased any worry you had as to what your financial position would be should he die before you, as was to be expected in view of the difference in ages between you.'

'He didn't.'

'When did you first learn that his company was in trouble?'

'He never mentioned that until . . . until I said I needed something in the kitchen.'

'What was that?'

'A self-cleaning oven.'

'What was his response?'

'He swore at me.'

'That alerted you to the trouble?' Jarvis was surprised and mystified; at least, that was what his tone of voice suggested.

'He told me I couldn't have anything because he was going to lose the company, he'd have to sell my car, he'd be left with little or no capital . . . and he cursed at me for wanting luxuries when he was facing disaster.'

'When exactly did this happen?'

'I don't remember exactly.'

'A few months before he died?'

'It might have been.'

'How would you describe your feelings when you learned the future you faced? Were you frightened?'

'Of course I was.'

'As your husband would have been. Yet, facing disaster, he asked Mr Linton to paint your portrait.'

'He wasn't thinking straight.'

'You tried to dissuade him?'

'How could I when he had already spoken to Mike?'

'You did not consider your husband's position rather than an artist's disappointment?' Jarvis paused for a while. 'Mrs Cane, we have heard that Mr Linton demanded he paint your portrait in his studio which, as the photos of it show, is far from salubrious. Your house would have proved a far more comfortable studio.'

'He explained that it helps an artist to have familiar things around him. It was his first commissioned portrait, and he didn't want anything to distract him from painting well.'

'"Distractions." A husband who might suddenly return home?'

'John was at work almost all the time, so it wouldn't make any difference whether I was there or at the studio.'

'But at home you employ part-time labour who will note what goes on; despite a lack of friends, an acquaintance might call. Having met Mr Linton, did you soon become friends?'

'Yes, but not—' She stopped.

'It clearly was a friendship which flourished.'

'And remained *just* a friendship.'

'Did Mr Linton never suggest he would welcome something more than mere friendship?'

'No.'

'Would you have found that welcome?'

'I am . . . I was married.'

'Despite the unfortunate consequences of your husband's illness, you did not seek sunnier times?'

'John was my husband.'

'When at the studio, was there physical contact between you and Mr Linton?'

'No.'

'You were, by your account, good friends, yet there was no greeting on your arrival?'

'We cheek-kissed.'

'That is not physical contact?'

'Not in the sense you were meaning.'

'What is your interpretation of what I meant?'

'You keep trying to suggest we were intimate. We were not.'

'Do you know the place called Devil's Dyke?'

'Yes.'

'At one point, there is a ledge part of the way down it on one side. Have you ever driven down on to that ledge?'

'No.'

'You did not do so on the fourteenth of October?'

'No.'

'Mr Linton did; also, the owner of a white Volvo. Do you still deny that was your Volvo and you were driving it?'

'Yes.'

'What if I tell you someone saw you drive down on to the ledge on that day? That the driver of the white Volvo was seen to leave the car and engage in a long and passionate embrace with Mr Linton? Will that enable you to remember the occasion?'

The judge said: 'You have not called such witness.'

'No, My Lord.'

'Then you will not suppose either the witness or his evidence.'

Jarvis was satisfied the jury would accept what had been alleged; nevertheless, he silently again referred to the judge in highly uncomplimentary terms.

SEVENTEEN

Closing speeches were made. Counsel repeated evidence in favour of the prosecution or defence, explained why evidence contrary to their cause was nonsense. Jarvis had the easier task. By the time he sat down, the afternoon was well advanced. The judge consulted the clerk of the court. He would not sum up until the next morning.

Linton emptied the last of the gin into the glass, added some tonic. He drank. Gin solved nothing, yet for a short, desirable moment, it provided the false suggestion it could. Even Micawber would not have suggested the summing-up could be favourable to Elaine. Evidence falsely named her to be a woman who, on the spur of the moment, had assisted her drunken husband to his death. Had there been evidence of premeditation, the charge would have been murder. When the jury returned to court and gave their verdict, the judge would impose sentence. Several years' imprisonment.

Linton slumped down on the bed in his studio and stared at the portrait of Elaine. A struggling artist could no longer ignore life by enjoying the 'pleasures' of a Bohemian life. Rising prosperity and the accompanying increase in prices meant even half a pint of beer was very expensive relative to the money he had. Elaine had brought colour to his life. The law was about to erase all that colour in the name of justice. His desperate need to help her, the impotency of anything he could do, tortured him as effectively as had once the knowledge that Elaine would never break her marriage vows.

He left the bed, tried to pour himself another drink, found the bottle was empty. Even the desire to drink himself into oblivion was thwarted. He returned to the bed, stared at the portrait and, born by a light mental breeze, an idea floated into his mind. He contemptuously dismissed it. It returned.

*   *   *

The nearest street light was several yards away and did little to dispel the darkness. 'What the hell's up?' Betty demanded as she stepped into the studio. 'Has the electricity fused?'

'I was just thinking.' He stood, switched on the bedside light. 'Thanks for coming.'

'Do you want to undress me, Mike, or shall I just strip?'

'There's no call for that.'

'Then why ask me to come here?'

'When you last left, you said something of which I didn't take any notice, but since then I've wondered what you meant.'

'You don't want to shag me, you just want to *ask* me something?'

'I hope that doesn't annoy you?'

'Not really.'

He wasn't sure she meant it; she looked upset. He put his arm around her and led her to the bed; they sat. 'But for Elaine, I'd have your clothes off in two seconds flat.'

'You're not saying that because—'

'I mean it.'

She nestled against him. 'Then I'll take a rain check.' She raised his right hand to cup her breast. Certain that to remove it abruptly would distress her, he left it in place. 'As you were leaving last time, you said: if only you were like Terry, but you're not. What did that mean?'

'Me wishing I could suggest something that'd help.'

'Who's Terry?'

'A bloke I knew when I was living in London in an area where if you heard someone had gone on a holiday, you knew he was doing a stretch. He was a country blagger – find a house that was unoccupied in the daytime and he'd be in and out of it with anything worth carrying. The police got on to him, but he'd enough insurance stowed away to buy a couple who swore on ten bibles he was with them when he was supposed to be doing a house in the countryside. They had to let him go free. He did another place that night to put two fingers up at 'em.'

'Didn't the police suspect the witnesses were lying?'

'Course they did. But suspect all they like, if they can't prove, it don't mean nothing.'

'So if *I* could find someone—'

'For Christ's sake, Mike! Try that and they'd have you inside before you could blink.'

'But if he got away with it because the two lied success-fully . . .?'

'You think they risked themselves for peanuts? Have you got ten thousand loose ones? Even if you had, where would you go looking for someone to back you?'

'Perhaps you could help me find a couple, or maybe three, who—?'

'And help you get your throat cut. Wake up, Mike. Even the way you talk says you don't come from the kind of life for that sort of thing. They'd think you was setting them up. And if you did find two right mugs, what then?'

'If the court accepted their evidence . . .'

'With them who they are and you who *you* are? Might as well shout from the rooftops that you've bunged them to lie for you. Afterwards, they'd squeeze you dry to keep their mouths latched; then, when you was skint, they'd make sure you couldn't try to get your own back by shopping them, if you catch my drift.'

'You think I'm hopelessly naive.'

'No, Mike, just someone who's desperate because he's losing someone very precious.'

When the wind was from the south, the sound of the bells of St Michael's reached Springside Road. Linton heard two o'clock strike as he stared up at his bedroom ceiling, which was patterned by street light which came through the threadbare curtains. Betty had provided fresh hope even as she had destroyed hope.

If an innocent man knew he was going to be shot, hanged, garrotted, lethally injected, did disbelief add to the torment or lessen it? Did he call on God, whether he believed or not, to grant a miracle? Did he ever understand and accept that injustice was part of life? . . . Did a young man who studied at some length the lascivious painting of a nude woman give more than a passing glance at her face?

As the church clock chimed four times, he got out of bed, dressed, left his flat and drove back to the studio. There, he painted an imag-ined naked Elaine in the posture in which Betty had been when Ted had brought the pizza and admired the current painting. He thought

– he hoped – that Ted, who was young and callow, would see no discernible difference between the painting of Betty and that of Elaine. In all the basic elements that a young man might be expected to notice – pose, general size of breasts, arrangement and colour of pubic hair – the paintings were alike. After a brief pause to consider, he added a barely discernible scar on the abdomen.

'Can I help at all?'

Linton had driven into town as soon as the shops were open. Luckily, the town had an abundance of cheap high-street jewellery stores and pawn shops, but this was the fourth he had tried and he was getting anxious. It was a small, independent store, packed to the gills with jewellery, from tasteful to tasteless. He suspected that the shop's motto might be 'something for every budget'.

Who would have thought that finding something so simple would be such a task? But there, in a crammed cabinet, was something that would do the job to perfection. Paranoia guided his every move; he tried not to indicate to the salesman, who was perhaps also the shop's owner, that he had spotted it.

'I've just come in to get the battery in my watch replaced,' he said. 'Will you do it while I wait?'

'Certainly,' the salesman said.

Linton wandered around the store, saving the cabinet containing the brooch until last.

'Here you are, sir,' the man said after some time. 'Can I help you with anything else?'

'This brooch has caught my eye,' Linton said, trying not to sound eager. 'I wonder . . .'

It did not take long to haggle the salesman down to an affordable price; he seemed eager to be rid of it, and Linton noted that there were two identical brooches in the cabinet. It was evidently not a popular piece.

He walked out of the shop, feeling as if he was on air.

Elaine had been allowed to have her mobile with her. Linton rang her and explained what he proposed. Suddenly more worried about his position than her own, she repeatedly begged him to forget the idea.

*   *   *

Linton drove past police divisional headquarters in Westhurst and had to continue for a quarter of a mile before he was able to park. He walked back, past the ugly commercial buildings which had replaced the market square; the public library with tired, broadleaved bushes around two of its sides; the three tall, large Victorian houses, their interiors now separated into apartments and offices. As he approached the headquarters, his rate of walking slowed, his thoughts tumbled around each other. What if . . .? Might the police . . .? Perhaps Betty would say . . .

The young constable behind the desk in the front room watched Linton enter. One more piffling complaint, he thought. One more stupid request or appeal for information.

'My name is Mike Linton.'

'Yes?'

It was clear the name meant nothing to the constable. A reminder of the insignificance of the case to almost everyone but Elaine and himself. 'I'd like a word with the inspector.'

'Which one?'

'Inspector Bell.'

'*Detective* Inspector Bell. Your reason for wanting to speak to him?'

'It's in connection with the case against Mrs Cane.'

'One moment, please.' The constable went into the communication office behind the desk, closed the door.

After a couple of minutes, he came out. 'Detective Inspector Bell is not available, but you can have a word with Detective Sergeant Hopkins. If you'll wait over there.' He pointed to a small alcove with side benches and a table on which were ancient magazines, police pamphlets and a well-thumbed notice listing the rights of the public when dealing with the police.

Hopkins eventually came around a corner and, at a nod from the constable, into the alcove.

'Good morning, Mr Linton. You want a word with Inspector Bell, but he's in court. How can I help you?'

'I want to report something which is very important.'

'We'll go along to one of the interview-rooms.'

By chance, it was the same room in which Linton had been questioned.

'I'll switch on the gubbins.' Hopkins did so, recorded date, time, and those present, even though certain he was about to be told something of no consequence; a police officer soon learned to record everything which could be recorded, or someone would always later deny that what he said had been said. 'You wish to say something in connection with the trial of Mrs Cane?'

'Yes.'

'As that is still in progress and you have given your evidence, I have to tell you that it may be very inadvisable for you to say anything.'

'I must.'

'Very well.'

'Mrs Cane was in my studio when her husband died.'

Hopkins stared at Linton for several seconds, then switched off the tape recorder without recording time or reason. 'I'm going to say something when by rights I should keep my mouth shut, Mr Linton, but I don't need to be told how you feel, seeing Mrs Cane on trial. So I'll remind you that however distressed you are, however desperately you want to help her, you will be guilty of trying to pervert the course of justice if you do not deny the claim you have just made or if you insist on repeating it.' He switched the recorder on. 'Will you repeat what you have just said?'

'Your forensic expert estimated Mr Cane's time of death as around half past two. But at that time, Mrs Cane was in my studio.'

'At what time did she arrive there?'

'It was mid morning.'

'When did she leave?'

'Around four thirty.'

'Why have you not mentioned this before?'

'Because . . .' He became silent.

'If what you have just told me is true, you should have given such evidence the moment there seemed to be a suggestion Mrs Cane was in any way involved in her husband's death.'

'You don't understand.'

'Then please explain.'

'She wasn't in the studio to sit for her portrait.'

'Why was she there?'

'Because of what had happened at her home.'

'She has constantly claimed that on leaving her house, after the unfortunate assault from her husband, she drove around the countryside.'

'After the argument with her husband, she came to my studio.'

'Why?'

'She needed emotional help. I tried to give that, and . . .'

'Yes?'

'We ended up making love.'

'You had sex with Mrs Cane?'

'If you must put it so bluntly.'

'You have repeatedly denied on oath that you were more than friendly with Mrs Cane.'

'I had to. Had it been known what our relationship had become, it was going to seem obvious she would want to be with me, not her husband, and then . . .'

'You understand that to lie when on oath is to commit perjury?'

'Yes.'

'Detective Inspector Bell will be informed of what you have told me and will decide the action to take.' Hopkins switched off the tape recorder. 'I'm sorry things have turned out as they have.'

Linton accepted the friendly words as evidence Hopkins sympathized with what he was trying to do, but wondered if he'd made a ridiculous mistake. There could be only one outcome – Elaine would be sent to jail for manslaughter, he for perjury.

EIGHTEEN

Morgan hurried into the CID general room. 'This'll blow your tits off.' Then, seeing only Lewis was present, added: 'Maybe it won't. Linton's come up with the story that his bit of nookie was in the studio when her old man took a dive.'

'Well I'm damned!' Lewis exclaimed. 'So I've been right from the beginning. She didn't help him over the banisters since she wasn't there. Her husband gave her hell, but she remained faithful. I've always said she's that kind of a person.'

'Then tell me why she was in Linton's studio.'

'He was working on her portrait, touching it up.'

'It's not that kind of touching he was enjoying.'

'You're trying to say . . . Impossible!'

'It's people like you who rush after rainbows with buckets and spades.'

'Yes?' said Harmsworth.

Bell drew the receiver slightly away from his ear. The detective chief superintendent raised his voice when irritated.

'There's a problem in the Cane case,' Bell said.

'Someone's ballsed-up a statement and got the judge shouting?'

'Linton came into the station, spoke to my sergeant and claims Mrs Cane was in his studio at the time of her husband's death.'

'All we bloody needed!'

'I've asked him to be brought in for questioning.'

'Phone me back when you have explained to him that a false alibi is worth ten years inside, so would he like to think again?'

Linton was shown into an interview room, similar to the previous one except that the form listing the rights of those being questioned was clean. Bell and Hopkins entered.

'Mr Linton,' Bell said, once they were all seated, 'I have read a transcript of the recording of the conversation you had with Sergeant Hopkins.' He tapped the opened folder on the table. 'Do you wish to withdraw or amend anything you said in the interview?'

'No.'

'You claim Mrs Cane unexpectedly came to your studio on Tuesday, the twelfth of October, at around eleven in the morning.'

'That is correct.'

'Was anyone else in the studio when she arrived?'

'No.'

'Did anyone turn up whilst she was there?'

'No.'

'She left when?'

'A considerable time later.'

'Can you verify any of your statements?'

'Mrs Cane will confirm all I've said.'

'As the evidence is of such importance to her, you will under-stand her confirmation may not carry much weight.'

'You are calling both of us liars?'

'If what you have just told us is true, what you have previously said in court proves you have constantly lied.'

'She was in my studio.'

'Your claim has been noted.'

'And automatically disbelieved?'

'Have you anything more you wish to say?'

'A sermon-full, but it won't do any good.'

'Then we will bring this meeting to an end.' Bell prepared to turn off the tape recorder.

Linton, about to stand, said: 'Hang on. You asked if anyone had come to the studio when Mrs Cane was there. I've just remembered. The pizza lad arrived at about half past two.'

Bell sat. 'You have, perhaps, forgotten the name of the firm who made the pizza and the name of the lad who delivered it?'

'His name is Ted, but I've no idea Ted what. The firm is called Amato Pizzas.'

'Is there any way of pinpointing that day?'

'How am I supposed to do that?'

'Something unusual happened, something was different. Why should he remember delivering a certain pizza, when he delivers pizzas for a career?'

'Elaine was in the changing area, but I think Ted may have overheard us talking. He probably presumed that she was my regular model, Betty, and that suited me fine. Elaine was concerned that she had lost something, and she had me searching for it.'

'You understand we shall be making enquiries?'

'I should not expect you to believe anything I say until you're forced to accept it. There's nothing more to tell you, so I'll leave.' He left.

Bell switched off the tape recorder.

'Has he pulled out the plum?' Hopkins suggested.

'No. And until we prove he's a quixotic fool, the DCS will be shouting for us to use thumbscrews.'

In the window of the pizzeria was a notice, bordered in Italian colours, which listed the pizzas one could choose and eat in the restaurant, takeaway, or have delivered to one's home; they were made by Arturo Amato, who had learned the art of producing the perfect pizza in San Pietro, Tapallo.

'Are you better known to the locals as Roger Milland?' Bell asked as he and Hopkins stood in a small office with a glass wall through which one could see the pizzas being produced.

'Helps trade to show an Italian name,' Milland answered. His round face was split by a moustache of considerable length; his figure showed he was a man who enjoyed his own product. 'Inspector, if the trouble is with the cockroaches—'

'I'm a police, not a bug inspector.'

'Sorry, I just was thinking—'

'Do you have a delivery lad by the name of Ted?'

'That's right.'

'We want a word with him.'

'What's he been up to?'

'We don't yet know. Is he here?'

Milland looked at his watch. 'Won't be for fifteen minutes.'

'Where's he live?'

'Brexton.'

'Then we'll remain until he arrives. It won't upset you.' That was a statement, not a question.

'Of course it won't, Inspector. Perhaps you would like to have something to eat while you wait?'

'I won't, but I expect my sergeant will.'

'Then please go into the restaurant and order what you want.'

Ted arrived as Hopkins finished his olive, tomato and cheese pizza. They spoke to him in the office. He tried to express disdain for authority, merely succeeded in looking slightly shady in character.

'Have a seat,' Bell said.

Ted sat, nervously fiddled with his T-shirt on which was printed 'Go to hell, love isn't rationed there'.

'Do you know Mr Linton, who has an artist's studio in Rackley Mill?'

Ted weighed up the possible dangers in answering. 'I've delivered there,' he finally admitted.

'On the twelfth of October?'

'Couldn't say.'

'Will there be a record of your deliveries on that day?'

'Likely. The old bast . . . Mr Milland writes everything down, like even when I'm a couple of minutes late because of the traffic.'

'Ask him to check if you made a delivery that day to Mr Linton.'

Ted moved slowly in order to show he wasn't going to be pushed around by authority. He was away for less than five minutes; he returned accompanied by Milland.

'I will need to look in the book to tell you what you want to know, Inspector,' Milland said.

'Then if you'll look?'

He went over to the desk, picked up a large orders diary, turned the pages, ran a finger half way down one. 'Mr Linton ordered a four-cheese pizza which was delivered that day at around half past two.'

'Around half past? Can you be more specific?'

'Unfortunately, no.' He shrugged. 'The state of traffic . . . the speed that Ted drove at . . .' He shrugged again.

'That's all, then.'

Milland hesitated.

'We'd like to have a word with Ted on his own.'

He left.

'Ted, can you fix that delivery in your mind?'

'Don't reckon,' he answered sullenly.

'Nothing unusual happened?'

'Can't remember nothing.'

'Was Mr Linton painting?'

'Always is, seeing as that's his job.'

'Was there a sitter there?'

'Most times there is.'

'Did you know who she was?'

'There's only the one – says he can't afford more.' Ted's manner changed. 'But she's a neat bit of crackling if you don't look at her face. But he puts a different head on her body and gets her in different positions. Once or twice you could see—'

'Concentrate on fixing the day in question in your mind. Seems you spent a long time looking at Mr Linton's painting.'

'You mean when she had her legs—'

'Probably. It's likely you didn't see her, but you may have heard her when she was getting dressed.'

'When she shouted she'd lost something? Made me think of what she'd of lost when she was at school.'

'D'you remember what she said she'd lost?'

'Her snakes. And . . . and . . . Mr Linton said he didn't know she'd brought her pythons, or something of the sort, with her.'

'Did you have any idea what they were talking about?'

'Sure. She'd lost her brooch.'

'How do you know that?'

'She told him, said he was being stupid suggesting real snakes.'

'Did she find her brooch?'

'Can't say. Had to get a move on or I'd of been late and old Milly would've been shouting.'

'Did you see her whilst you were there?'

'Didn't need to, not with that painting.'

'Would you recognize that if you saw it again?'

'Would I forget winning the lottery?'

'I may well ask you to identify it later on and confirm it was what Mr Linton had been painting when you heard the woman in the changing room say she'd lost her brooch.'

'No problem, if Milly don't kick at me for not being at work.'

'We'll clear things with him. Thanks for your help.'

'Mike's in trouble, is he?'

'We can't say.'

'Bad luck if he is. Like I told him, I wouldn't mind his job. Her lying on the bed, straight offering it.'

'You're all for going to hell?'

'How's that . . .? Oh, my T-shirt. Smooth, ain't it?'

'Dangerously optimistic.'

Ted left.

'Things are never as straightforward as you want,' Hopkins said mournfully.

Bell and Morgan made their way to the consultation room. Their wait was short. Elaine was shown into the room; her accompanying policewoman left, carefully closing the door as she did so. Bell expressed their regret at the conditions at which they met again; she dismissed his concern in a tone which named hypocrisy.

They sat on opposite sides of a stained and scarred table, as hundreds of officers and those on trial had before.

'I'll be as brief as possible, Mrs Cane,' Bell said. 'Will you tell me where you were during the afternoon of Tuesday, the twelfth of October?'

'I've answered that a dozen and one times. After I escaped the house, I drove around the countryside.'

'I have reason to disbelieve you.'

'You never need reason; for you, disbelief comes automatically.'

'Fresh evidence has come to hand which, if proven, would be to your advantage. I will ask you again, where were you that afternoon?'

She did not answer for over a minute. When she did so, she spoke in a low voice. 'I was in Mike's studio.'

'Why were you there?'

'I . . . I was in such a state after what had happened, I had to be with someone.'

'Why Mr Linton?'

'Because I knew he'd help me.'

'In what way help you?'

'Comfort me.'

'Did he succeed?'

'He was so understanding that we . . .'

'Yes?'

'Things went further than . . . than we wanted.'

'Are you saying you indulged in sexual intercourse?'

'You make it sound so crude and nasty.'

'How would you describe it, Mrs Cane?'

'We made love.'

'What did you do afterwards?'

'I left his studio after he did the . . . the fun painting.'

'Would you like to explain?'

'Not really.'

'I need to know.'

'It's so embarrassing, and I'm certain you won't begin to understand.'

'I should like to try.'

'We'd been in love almost from the day we first met. Before

long, we both wanted . . . but didn't. When I went to the studio that day, I was in a state of shock and he had to comfort me and . . .' She was silent. Bell waited. 'When something wonderful happens one can become light-headed, want to play the fool, laugh at the world. Can you have the slightest idea what I mean?'

'I think so.'

'Mike said he wanted to paint a picture of me that would burst into flames from internal combustion. Do you now understand?'

'I'm afraid not, Mrs Cane.'

'He painted me like . . . like those other paintings.'

'Those he does for the magazine?'

'Yes. It was so quick; I was amazed at his talent.'

'What happened when it was finished?'

'I . . . I got dressed, of course.'

'Where?'

'In his studio. Where else?'

'In what part?'

'Where he calls the changing room.'

'Did anything unusual happen while you were dressing?'

'I don't know what you'd call unusual. Someone delivered a pizza, but is that unusual?'

'It can be. Please continue.'

'When I came out of the changing room, I told Mike he ought to do some cooking and eat more healthily.'

'Did you see the person who delivered the pizza?'

'No.'

'Was the person male or female?'

'Male.'

'You've just said you didn't know who it was.'

'Mike called him Ted.'

'Did you say anything while he was in the studio?'

'Probably not. Why should I?'

'You didn't ask Mr Linton anything?'

'There *was* something . . . I called out to Mike if he had seen my snakes. Being Mike, he said something about there not being any pythons in sight.'

'What did you mean?'

'I thought I'd lost my brooch because it wasn't in my handbag.'

'You are not wearing it now.'

'As you see. A roughness had developed at one point. Only tiny, but irritating. I thought I'd put it in my handbag to take to a jeweller's to get it sorted out, but hadn't.'

'Will you describe it?'

'Whatever for?'

'It may be important.'

'It's made of silver, a low grade I was told, and it's two snakes entwined about each other.'

'It sounds to be an unusual brooch.'

'Which is what caught my attention when my husband gave it to me before our marriage. Apparently, it's Indian and comes from a city somewhere in the north where they honour snakes. Seems a strange thing to honour when they cause so many deaths in the country.'

'Where is the brooch now?'

'At home.'

'I'd like to see it.'

'You only believe what you can see and touch?'

'In circumstances such as these, yes.'

'Then you want me to get it?'

'I think that is not possible. I need your permission to go to Gill Tap and see it. May I have that permission?'

'I can't think why you have to see it, why you're even interested in it, but if you must, satisfy yourselves, ask Mike to show it to you.'

'It will need someone else to do so.'

'Ever suspicious! Mrs Owen won't be there, but you can call in at her place and ask if she'll be kind enough to let you into Gill Tap. She has a key.'

'Do you know whereabouts the brooch will be?'

'In the top right-hand drawer of the dressing-table in our – in what was our – bedroom. It has no real value, so I didn't bother to put it in the safe.'

'Why did you not go back to wearing it after you thought you had lost it?'

'I still haven't found time to have the roughness erased.'

Mrs Owen expressed her thoughts concerning the police before she reluctantly showed them into the large bedroom. When Bell opened the top drawer of the dressing-table, she watched with much concentration to make certain what he did.

He picked up the brooch. Two silver snakes were entwined around each other in opposite directions so that their mouths faced each other, jaws open.

Bell thanked Mrs Owen for her help. She said something forcefully, but spoke too softly for them to understand.

They returned to the car. As he settled behind the wheel, Morgan said: 'Mrs Cane's a lot smarter than I thought. Had even you on the run, guv.'

'A junior's opinion of his senior may be welcome in your half of the world, but in this half, it bloody well isn't.'

NINETEEN

L inton heard footsteps of two people on the wooden stairs. Bell and a sidekick? Bloodhounds following a false scent which they must be made to believe was genuine. His inner tension increased. Guilt could be proved by what one did not do. Had he ignored or forgotten anything; failed to appreciate how fatal to Elaine and himself one small detail would be?

'Evening,' Bell said as he entered the studio, followed by Morgan. To have announced their presence before entering would have allowed Linton to think he was still in some degree in control of the situation. 'I hope you'll forgive the interruption?'

'So long as it helps sort everything out, you're welcome.'

'It may or it may not do that.'

'I'll get the chairs.' He set them by the bed. 'I was thinking of making myself coffee, so would you like some?'

'I won't, thanks.'

'And you?' he asked Morgan.

'Never say no, like the girls on Bondi.'

Linton switched on the kettle which was on the floor, set out two mugs on a tray which had originally pictured a swirling group of horses, now showed nothing identifiable.

'Mrs Cane will have told you we have spoken to her,' Bell said.

'What makes you think that?'

'You want to give me the trouble of again tracking her mobile phone calls?' he asked lightly.

'Never believe in giving anyone trouble.' Linton spooned instant coffee into the cups.

'You'll also know what she told us, since she'll have said what you suggested she did. When did she arrive here on the twelfth?'

'She couldn't remember what I supposedly said?'

'Her evidence needs to be corroborated.'

'And my answer will do that?'

'It will show you both give the same one.'

'Do you like sugar and milk?'

'Please.'

He returned to the cupboard. 'I hope you'll excuse the non-U service?'

'A long time since I last heard that expression.'

'It's become politically incorrect to infer behaviour follows breeding.' He carried the tray across, held it for Morgan to help himself to sugar and milk, sat on the bed.

'We've had a word with Ted,' Bell said.

Linton added sugar to his coffee. 'Presumably that's Ted of the long hair and youthful liking of the ladies.'

'When he last delivered here, at around half past two on the Tuesday in question, he says a woman was in the dressing room.'

'Mrs Cane. Didn't he tell you that?'

'Since he didn't see her, he can't identify her.'

'Not directly, but he heard her speak to me.'

'He heard a woman speak.'

'Didn't he tell you Mrs Cane had asked me if I'd seen her brooch?'

'Ted could have had no idea who was speaking. You will not expect us to overlook the fact that if Mrs Cane was here when her husband died, the charge of manslaughter is invalid. Since she was not, the way of trying to prove otherwise is to convince others that the speaker was Mrs Cane. I'm sufficiently unconvinced to believe the lady was your model.'

'Ingenious, but hopelessly off-track. Betty will tell you she was not here.'

'You paint other models than this Betty, of course.'

'If I could, since variety is the spice of painting, but I cannot afford such luxury.'

'I want Betty's surname and address.'

'It's Fowler. I don't know where she lives, except it's to the east of the town.'

'Is she married?'

'I have never asked.'

'You had been painting Mrs Cane before Ted brought the pizza?'

'Correct.'

'Since she was in the changing room, that suggests she needed to dress.'

'Of course.'

'And posed for you in the nude. But she presents herself as a woman who would not wish to do such a thing.'

'You've captured her character exactly. I imagine she was too embarrassed to describe the circumstances which resulted in such uncharacteristic behaviour?'

'She did say something which surprised me. Do you have the painting of her you made that day?'

'Yes.'

'I should like to see it.'

'You really expect me to show you something so personal to her and me? Yet I suppose if I don't, you'll not accept what did happen.'

He went over to where he kept canvases, paints, brushes, palette knives and books he used for reference. He returned, handed the small painting to Bell, who briefly studied it, passed it to Morgan.

'You say the woman in this painting is Mrs Cane?' Bell asked.

'I do.'

'I very much doubt she would ever be recognized from it.'

'Naturally.'

'You accept the visual likeness is slight?'

'Of course.'

'You understand the significance of that?'

'No.'

'It is very probable that this is a painting of Betty Fowler and you are only saying the subject is Mrs Cane because that would support your claim she was here in the studio at the very time of her husband's death.'

'From what you've just said, you're probably going to question Betty to find out if she was here.'

'And even if she confirms what you say, her confirmation will be treated with the greatest reserve.'

'How does one persuade you that she is telling the truth? By collecting four bishops who swear she is?'

'In the face of the evidence, I would find myself doubting even them.'

'You're convinced I'm lying when I say the woman in this painting is Mrs Cane?'

'I have not made that obvious?'

'Look at the abdomen below the right breast.'

Bell studied the area.

'What do you see?'

'Nothing unusual.'

'Look again.'

After a moment, Bell said: 'There is a small mark.'

'A scar. When she was young, Mrs Cane had a nasty fall which resulted in a fairly serious injury. That scar is the unwanted memory of it. Unless you can present another woman I have painted who has a scar of the same size in the same position on the body, you'll have to accept it was she whom I had painted when Ted brought the pizza and my "model" had lost her brooch.'

'I should like to have the painting for a while.'

'Provided you don't identify the sitter when you pass it around.'

'It will be shown only to those who need to see it. It will be returned to you as soon as it is proved Mrs Cane bears a similar scar.'

'And you will unwillingly have to accept she could not have had any part in her husband's death.'

'I never answer for the future.'

'Nor do I. Which is why, until recently, I have never understood how simple truths can be turned into complicated lies.'

The two detectives left.

In the car, as Morgan fixed his seat belt he said: 'As slippery as an eel. I don't think you—'

'If you want to return to walking a beat, just tell me what you think.'

Elaine and a policewoman were in the court conference room.

Bell and another man entered; the policewoman left. Bell wished Elaine a good morning, said: 'Dr Fraiche is here, Mrs Cane, to examine you if you consent.'

'I should consult my own doctor if I thought that necessary,' she answered.

'I will explain.'

'There is something left that needs explanation?'

'Both you and Mr Cane have said you were in his studio at the time of your husband's death. If true, you cannot be guilty of having had any part in his death. Will you permit Dr Fraiche to examine your body to determine whether there is a scar in a certain place?'

'If it will help make you finally understand the truth, I'll be glad for him to do so.'

'PC Haslit and I will be outside, so there can be no fear of your being disturbed. The doctor will tell me when his examination is over.'

Bell left the room, nodded at the PC who was standing nearby, made his way out of the building and lit a cigarette as he stood at the top of the grandiose and unnecessary steps which led down to street level.

PC Haslit came out of the building. 'The doctor's completed his examination, sir.'

'And?'

'Mrs Cane has a faint scar on her abdomen, and he confirms that it is very similar in size and position to the one visible on the painting of her.'

He returned into the building, went down to the consultation-room, spoke to the doctor, thanked him for his help.

'Satisfied?' Elaine demanded when they were on their own.

He sat opposite her. 'Mrs Cane, as you will now know, the scar you bear seems to confirm, as Mr Linton has told me, that it was you in the dressing room when Ted, the pizza lad, called at the studio.'

'Confirmation obviously very reluctantly accepted.'

'There are, however, one or two points to discuss.'

'As always!'

'The face in the painting does not entirely resemble yours.'

'We were acting crazily, or, as you'd no doubt say, perversely . . .' She stopped.

'I should not express such an opinion.'

'You actually can understand we were acting as if . . . as if we were drunk or high on drugs?'

He said nothing.

'When we had . . . calmed down, I suppose is one way of putting it, he altered the face a little so that no one would be able to identify me positively as the sitter.'

'Then why didn't he erase the scar?'

'I can't answer that.'

'If both of you wanted to make certain no one could ever see the painting and identify you, why didn't one of you destroy it?'

'I can't answer that either. But perhaps, from his point of view, it's akin to a man who is going to be away from his girl for a while, keeping a piece of her inner clothing as a warm memory.'

'Your imagination is no less active than Mr Linton's,' he said.

An hour later, Bell was in his room when Morgan entered. 'Yes?' Bell asked.

'Has the doc checked Mrs Cane for scars?'

'Yes. She has a faint one in the right place.'

'You know, guv, one has to take one's hat off to those two.'

'Clear off back to Wongawongaland.'

TWENTY

Morgan entered the detective sergeant's room. 'I've nailed Betty Fowler, sarge.'

'Then unnail her and question her.'

'It's meant to be clocking-off time for me, and I've already—'

'Right now, time off duty is an unaffordable luxury.'

'But I've arranged to meet a sheila and drive down to the coast and have supper!'

'Then she'll go hungry and save her reputation.'

'A policeman's lot is not a happy one.'

'Start singing and you'll be on night duty for the next year.'

Morgan left, went down to the ground floor, out to the parking space and over to a CID car. He drove to 56a Lecton Park, a deceitful name for a characterless house in a characterless area.

Betty's flat was on the top floor of one of several 1920 houses, built for, and in honour of, returned heroes of World War I who could seldom afford to buy one.

'Yes?' Betty said as she stood in the half-open doorway.

He introduced himself.

'What's the problem this time?'

'There isn't one. I just need a quick word.'

She hesitated, shrugged her shoulders, turned and went into a sitting room which would seem crowded if three persons were present. He followed, his thoughts sombre. To possess a body which started a man's mind on a ten-second hundred yard dash, but a face which brought it to a halt, showed nature at its most vicious.

They sat on two chairs which had led a hard life. He said: 'Let's have a chat about the twelfth of October.'

'I can never remember any yesterdays.'

She was fiddling with the solitaire diamond ring on her finger. If genuine, he would have asked her from whom she'd nicked it. 'What did you do that afternoon?'

'Went to Buckingham Palace for tea.'

'Did Phillip give you a wink? . . . Come on, the quicker I know, the quicker I can ask if you're busy when I get some time off.'

'Trust me, I'm busy.' She picked up a pack of cigarettes, tapped one out, lit it. 'I watched the telly.'

'You were at Linton's studio, giving him an eyeful.'

'Yeah? Want to tell me what more I wasn't doing?'

'He had painted you when someone turned up. Like to say who that was?'

'Lost my memory when I was hit on the head with a tomahawk.'

'Ted, a pizza delivery lad with long hair and pimples. He says you were there.'

'Then he's been eating too many pizzas.'

'He heard you talking to Linton while you were dressing. You told him you'd lost your snakes brooch.'

'Don't do snakes. Horrible things.'

'Then why wear a brooch with 'em?'

'I said, I don't *do* 'em. You got wax in your ears?'

'Suppose we get a warrant to search this place?'

'You won't find anything worth stealing.'

'Try thinking what's best for you and forget the rest, or you'll end up in court on a charge of perjury.'

'And if that don't work, you'll try me for running a knocking shop?'

'You know what perjury will cost? I don't want to see you inside.'

'Can't say the same about you.'

'It's not worth the risk. Come clean and give your conscience a break.'

'I wasn't working because Mike didn't want me, Ed is getting it off in the south of France and Bert's found a model who can fling her tits over her shoulders.'

'You don't want to listen to reason?'

'Never get the chance when you lot are around.'

'What did you say when you found you'd lost your snakes brooch?'

'Snakes alive.'

'Ted recognized your voice. That calls you a liar.'

'Brought the handcuffs?'

'I'm trying to make things easy for you.'

'Won't get you a free humping.'

He left.

Bell listened to Morgan's report. He picked up a pencil and drew meaningless shapes on the sheet of paper in front of him. 'Will gentle pressure persuade her to change her evidence?'

'If you ask me—'

'It takes you time to realize that's what I'm doing?'

'I reckon she'll stick to her story unless you tie her to a stake and pile wood around her. She's as tough as a Queensland cane-cutter.'

Bell drew two more shapeless shapes. He looked up. 'I want Mr Allun and Miss Fowler here midday tomorrow.'

Betty opened the front door of her flat to face Morgan. 'Move on two houses and you'll get half an hour for a tenner if you wash first.'

'I'm here because I like quality.'

'Then stay away from mirrors.'

'Someone had to have a word with you, so I volunteered. I'm asking you to come along to the station by twelve tomorrow.'

'You arresting me?'

'Perish the thought.'

'Then get stuffed.'

'Inspector's orders.'

'Tell *him* to get stuffed.'

'A car will pick you up and return you afterwards.'

'After what?'

'That's up to you.'

'What do they want me for?'

'A chat.'

'About what?'

'How you spend your time.'

'With honest company, when I'm allowed.'

'They can't all be as straight as me. The car will be along at eleven forty. I'll tell the driver that if it's rained, he's to put his coat down on the pavement for you to get into the car.'

'Sod off.' She slammed the door shut.

Ted entered the front room at divisional HQ, removed his crash helmet, moved to the desk. PC Yeo came out of the communications room, stared at Ted. 'What's brought you here? Riding without a licence and insurance, or persuading a fourteen year old she needs a tantric massage?'

'How do *I* know why I had to come? My boss just said.'

'So who are you?'

'Ted Allun.'

'Maybe the sarge knows more than I do.' He used the internal telephone.

Ted, nervous and apprehensive, recalled a couple of reasons from the past which might explain why the police had called him to the station. As the minutes passed, he recalled a few more.

A PC came round the corner. 'Allun?'

'Yeah.'

He was shown into an interview-room. He had recently seen a film in which the victim had sworn by all the saints he did not know what he was supposed to have done and had been beaten unconscious for his ignorance.

A curly-headed, broad-shouldered, strongly-featured man entered. 'Allun?'

He nodded.

'I'm Detective Constable Morgan.'

Ted silently feared they had found out about—

'I've not been near the news, so what was the final score at the Gabba?'

'What . . . what d'you mean?' Ted muttered, fearful of the consequences of not understanding.

'Don't you know what goes on at the Gabba?'

'Never heard of it.'

That was the end of conversation until Bell entered in a rush, switched on the tape recorder, sat. 'On the twelfth of October, Allun, you delivered a pizza to Mr Linton in his studio at Rackley Mill.'

'I don't know what I did that—'

'Your boss has confirmed there was an order from Mr Linton on that day and you delivered it. Previously, you have described that while at the studio you saw a painting on which Mr Linton had been working. Is that correct?'

'Yeah, but it wasn't because she was almost—' He stopped.

'Perhaps the colouring caught your attention. Describe the painting.'

'It was a woman.'

'And?'

'She was showing two and one.'

'Translate.'

'Naked.'

'Was she standing or sitting?'

'Lying down.'

'Where?'

'On the bed.'

'How was she lying?'

'So you could almost see . . . you know.'

'Look at this painting. Do you recognize it?' Bell put the painting down on the table in front of Allun.

He barely glanced at it. 'That's her.'

'Do you recognize the painting in its entirety? Are you sure that's how she was lying; do you recognize the individual bits and pieces of the background?'

'Sure. Tell you, I wouldn't bother to watch porn if she was there.'

'Substantial confirmation. Was the model in sight?'

'What model?'

'The woman who Mr Linton had been painting.'

'She was in the changing room.'

'How do you know?'

'I heard her talking to him.'

'What did she say?'

'She'd lost her snakes.'

'What did he reply?'

'Said something about pythons. So she told him it was her brooch she'd lost.'

'I have arranged for two women to come here. You will not see them, but you will listen to them when they speak, and afterwards I want you to say if you recognize one of their voices. You understand?'

Ted was silent.

'You speak a primitive language,' Bell said to Morgan. 'Sort him out while I go off and check things.'

Fifteen minutes later, Ted, accompanied by Morgan, was shown into the conference room; the door was left slightly ajar so that sound was not blocked, but vision was.

Elaine was asked to speak outside and say she had lost her snakes brooch, she had thought it was in her handbag, had Mike seen it. She left, in the company of a PC. Five minutes later, again unseen by Ted, Betty repeated the words.

Ted was asked: 'Did you recognize either voice as that of the woman you heard on the twelfth when you delivered the pizza to Mr Linton at Rackley Mill?'

'I dunno.'

'Think back and remember all you can about the way the woman spoke, her pronunciation. Did she rush the ends of her words, did she speak slowly or quickly, would you say she had an educated speech?'

'It ain't easy.'

'Try.'

'I think maybe it was the first one.'

'Can you be a little more definite?'

'It's just . . . But then it was maybe more like the second one. Only, the first one did talk a bit proper.'

If the future of the country rested on the youth of today, God help the country, Bell thought.

'Sir,' Bell said over the phone, 'unfortunately, we have been unable to prove the alibi a fabrication.'

The detective chief superintendent spoke sharply. 'Are you satisfied you have pursued all possible leads?'

'We have covered everything, and there has been no hint of conspiracy, no contradiction in the respective evidence to help prove there has been one.'

'You are prepared to accept Mrs Cane was in the studio at the time of her husband's death?'

'Forced, sir, not prepared.'

'Might Chief Inspector Jakes have more success?'

In Bell's opinion, and it was not only his, Jakes was boastful, incompetent and had gained promotion only through his readiness to take the credit for another's actions. 'To a witness, sir, a trial makes very clear the majesty and power of the law, and that often leaves him fearful and ready to tell the truth. If we produce the witnesses to the alibi, they will have to face the cross-examination of Mr Jarvis. That may do the trick.'

'And if it doesn't?'

Bell did not answer.

'What's the judge going to say when asked to allow the intro-duction of new evidence at this stage of the trial?'

'I doubt he can refuse.'

'You are not conversant with the reluctance of a judge to face novelty? Are you preparing a new file for the Crown Prosecution Service?'

'Yes, sir.'

'Make it very clear that the police cannot be blamed for this confusion.'

TWENTY-ONE

When Mr Justice Eveley spoke to Quinn, he did not try to hide his annoyance. 'I have been informed you wish to make a request?'

'Yes, My Lord. It is that I be allowed to introduce new evidence.'

'What is that evidence?'

'I have learned that the accused has an alibi, My Lord.'

'Are you aware that the defence, when introducing an alibi, has to provide the Crown Prosecution Service with full details of that alibi *before* trial, in order that the prosecution may examine the evidence in detail?'

Getting rid of some of his frustration, Quinn thought, by implying I might be ignorant of the rules.

'It is unusual for fresh evidence to be introduced at trial,' Mr Justice Eveley continued. 'It is *highly* unusual for the nature of that evidence to be an alibi. Mr Quinn, are you satisfied this alibi is not an attempt to evade justice?'

'Yes, My Lord.'

'In your judgement, is the admittance of the evidence essential to the course of justice?'

'Yes, My Lord.'

'In the circumstances, you are testing the strength of your judgement severely, and should that prove to be fallacious, the consequences might well be harmful to your career.'

A ten-year stretch without remission? 'My Lord, the facts of the alibi have only just been put forward, and there was no chance

of advising the prosecution as and when required. Yet it is my
understanding that the police have been able to question relevant
witnesses.'

The judge spoke to Jarvis. 'Does the prosecution accept that?'

Jarvis, who had hurried to his feet, untangled a corner of the
gown from around his legs. 'The officer concerned has assured
me an investigation has been carried out.'

'Thank you.'

Jarvis sat; the judge was silent for a while before he addressed
the jury. 'Fresh evidence is seldom allowed during a trial; it is
highly unusual indeed to be asked to allow the introduction of
an alibi. It is my duty to hold whether such evidence should be
admitted at this late stage of the trial. I have decided that the
demands of justice require it should be. Mr Quinn you will call
your witnesses.'

The jury, if not exactly aware of what was happening, showed
considerably more interest in the case than they had previously
done.

Betty was called and took the oath.

'Miss Fowler,' Quinn said after the preliminary questions had
been answered, 'where were you on the afternoon of the twelfth
of October?'

'I was at home.'

'I understand you are employed on a casual basis by the artist
Mr Linton.'

'Mike? That's right.'

'Why did you not attend Mr Linton's studio on the afternoon
in question?'

'He didn't want me that day, see? Mike said he couldn't afford
to hire me again until he'd been paid by his magazine. I ain't
working for free – I'm no mug!'

He took her through her evidence, hoping, as the judge's words
haunted his mind, that she would confirm she spoke the truth.

Jarvis cross-examined. 'You work for Mr Linton. Do you pose
for a number of artists?'

'Some.'

'Can you suggest a number?'

'Not really.'

'One might think that should be relatively easy.'

Jarvis had wanted to suggest that Linton's work was very necessary to her, raising the possibility she would support him when that might not be justified. She judged, however, that he was suggesting her facial features made it likely very few artists would wish to paint her; her embarrassed anger overcame her nervousness. 'Artists like my body, I'll have you know!'

'In what way?'

'You calling me a slag?'

The judge briefly leaned forward to speak to the clerk of the court. Many thought he was asking the meaning of 'slag'. He sat upright. 'Mr Jarvis, it might help the witness if you rephrase your question.'

'Miss Fowler, were you saying that artists appreciate the nature of your form?'

'Ain't no different from anyone else's.'

'By contemporary standards of obesity, it might seem welcomingly different to many.'

'Been thinking what I look like without me clothes on?'

A few noticed the judge's lips twitch.

'I have seen the photograph of your painting.'

The remark panicked Quinn; if she accepted it had been she who had posed for it . . .

'What one?'

Jarvis requested the witness be handed a photograph.

The judge said: 'Am I to see what the witness is being shown?'

'My Lord, I was about to ask that you be handed a copy of the photograph. Later, copies will be shown to the jury.'

The judge was given a photograph.

Betty looked at hers. 'That ain't me.'

Quinn regained his composure.

'There is reason to believe, Miss Fowler, that although the facial features are not yours, the body is.'

'Well, it ain't.'

'I put it to you that that is a lie, that you have every reason to know it is a photograph of a painting of your body.'

'The tits are wrong.'

'In what way do the breasts in the painting differ from yours?'

'Trying to get personal?'

'Miss Fowler,' the judge said, 'although you may well find

the question distasteful, counsel has the right to put it and you are under the obligation to answer.'

'From the look of him, he gets pleasure doing it.'

'You will not make remarks of such a nature.'

'He can call me a slag and I can't say he's—'

'You will take note of what I have just said, or you may become in contempt of court.'

Jarvis waited before he said: 'Would you explain the difference which convinces you that it is not a painting of you.'

'I said, her tits are wrong. Mine don't flop like hers are starting to do.'

'Is that not a matter of personal judgement and, perhaps, self-interest?'

'She don't look the kind to have ever had a twirly.'

'What is that?'

'You can't say, but you're supposed to know everything?'

'Miss Fowler,' the judge said, 'will you explain what a "twirly" is?'

'Like a Brazilian, only different.'

'Mr Jarvis, I fear I am none the wiser.'

'Perhaps if my learned friend were to speak to the witness and ask her to explain?'

'Very well.'

Quinn made his way to the end of the bench and across to the witness-box. He spoke to Betty, returned to his seat. 'My Lord, I understand some ladies have their pubic hairs shaved into forms different from those which nature provided. The "twirly" is one such. Miss Fowler assures me she enjoys such an alteration. As you will have observed, the person in the painting does not.'

Jarvis stood. 'My Lord, perhaps you may think it advisable to obtain medical confirmation of what we have just heard.'

'Is he saying I *ain't* got a twirly?' Betty demanded.

'Miss Fowler,' the judge said, 'it would greatly help this court if you would agree to be examined in order to confirm your statement.'

'So long as it ain't him what looks.' She indicated Jarvis.

'A doctor will be asked to do so.'

'That's all right, then.'

'My Lord,' Jarvis said, 'in the circumstances, perhaps the

accused may wish to help prove that the distinction is of the importance that the witness suggests.'

The judge spoke to Elaine. 'Mrs Cane, you have every right to refuse the suggestion; on the other hand, you may feel it would be to your advantage.'

'I will do anything to prove I'm innocent.'

'The court will not adjourn, but will remain in session while the examinations are carried out.'

Quinn reported to the judge. 'My Lord, Doctor Lodge confirms that Miss Fowler has had her pubic hairs altered into a pattern, while Mrs Cane has not.'

'Thank you. Mr Jarvis, do you wish to resume your cross-examination?'

Jarvis stood. 'Miss Fowler, when did you have the pattern sculpted?'

'Had it for months, ever since I got fed up with the Brazilian.'

'I suggest the change is very recent and was carried out in order to enable you to appear to be able to prove the painting was not of you.'

'If I told you you was on fire, you wouldn't believe me, would you?'

Jarvis sat.

Allun was called.

'Did you deliver a pizza to Mr Linton, at his studio, on the twelfth of October?' Quinn asked.

'Yes, sir.' Unlike Betty, Ted was overwhelmed by the visible and invisible majesty and menace of the courtroom, and by the bewigged legal officers.

'Will you tell the court what happened while you were in the studio.'

'I handed him the pizza – four cheeses. He paid and I cleared off.'

'Was Mr Linton on his own?'

'There was a woman in what he calls the changing room.'

'How do you know that?'

'Heard her call out to Mike, where was her snakes?'

'Did you understand what that meant?'

'Thought she was tight, like him when he said he couldn't see no pythons. Then she told him it was her brooch she couldn't find.'

'Did you see the woman in the changing room?'

'Not a sight.'

'Did you look at the painting Mr Linton had been working on?'

'Yeah.'

'Will you look at a photograph and say if the painting it shows was the one you saw that day?'

He was handed a photograph. He glanced at it quickly. 'That's her all right.'

'How can you be so certain?'

'Because . . . She . . . I mean . . . '

'Perhaps you wish to refer to the sitter's posture and her pubic hairs?'

'Yes,' Allun answered as, to his angry amazement, he blushed.

'Have you recently been asked to listen to the voices of two women, named to you as witness one and witness two, whom you could not see, in order to try to identify if one of them was the woman you had heard in the changing room that day?'

'Yes.'

'Did you name one?'

'Yeah.'

'Who was that?'

'One.'

'What made you choose her?'

'She talked proper.'

'That was the voice of Mrs Cane.'

Allun saw Quinn sit and, in a hurry to leave, turned. The nearby policeman in a low voice told him to stay.

Jarvis cross-examined. 'Did you have any doubts about your identification of the voice?'

'Might have done.'

'Why do you say that?'

'Well it . . . it wasn't easy. First off, I kind of thought it was the other one.'

'In fact, you first confidently named number two, did you not?'

'Yeah.'

'Who was Miss Fowler . . . Will you agree that, at best, you were and are uncertain as to which, if either, of the women you heard was the woman who had been in the studio and reported the loss of her brooch?'

'I suppose.'

Linton stepped into the witness-box, was reminded he was still on oath.

'Please tell the court what happened on the twelfth of October,' Quinn said.

Linton gave his evidence slowly, carefully.

Jarvis cross-examined. 'You have said Mrs Cane was distressed after she left her house that day, that she came to your studio because she was in love with you, and you with her, and you would be able to console her. Have you not assured the court more than once that you and she were not in love, were merely friends?'

'Yes.'

'You were lying?'

'If I'd admitted we were in love, this would have been thought to be further proof of Mrs Cane's guilt.'

'If you find it easy to lie when circumstances offer an advantage, why should we now believe any part of your evidence? Why should we believe you are even able to appreciate the meaning of "truth"?' He briefly paused. 'Have you previously denied you had a sexual relationship with Mrs Cane?'

'Yes.'

'More lies?'

'Given for the same reason.'

'The court will wonder how many further lies you have spoken and wish to dismiss with the same excuse. Having indulged in a sexual encounter with Mrs Cane – the first, you said, but can we believe that? – you painted her in the nude?'

'Yes.'

'Most would deem that to be extremely unusual post-coital behaviour.'

'I have tried to explain.'

'Without, I suggest, much success. I will refer to the painting you showed the police in order to substantiate your evidence.' Jarvis turned to face the bench. 'My Lord, because of its importance, the jury will need to study, as you have done, a photograph of the painting. However, due to its nature, would Your Lordship order that all copies be returned as soon as they are no longer essential to the evidence?'

'Are we to have no end to unusual requests . . .? Very well. Members of the jury, when handed copies of this painting, you will put them down on the shelving in front of yourselves and will return them when called upon to do so.'

Groves, a young reporter from the local newspaper, sent to cover the trial because the editor did not consider it likely to be of great interest, wondered how he could get hold of a copy and what tag-line to give it. The evidence gets the hots?

Photos were handed to the jury.

Jarvis asked: 'Mr Linton, do you wish to claim this to be a painting of Mrs Cane?'

'Yes. It *is* a painting of Mrs Cane.'

'I need to refer to certain matters which may cause the accused embarrassment and I apologize for this . . . Mrs Cane's form has to be judged as not that of someone who has suffered some of time's imperfections. The figure in your painting is of someone who has suffered no loss of youth.'

'Miss Fowler – Betty – did not think so. If there are differences, it is because I took artistic liberties.'

'What does that mean in everyday terms?'

'I erased a few of what some would call physical blemishes.'

'Does than not prevent your painting's being a true likeness?'

'It is true to character.'

'Would you expect someone viewing the face of the figure to identify her as Mrs Cane?'

'Probably not. I altered the facial features a little.'

'Why?'

'To avoid the chance of identification.'

'You were so elated by pleasure that you behaved in a manner, as you have admitted, many might find unacceptable, yet at the same time were sufficiently sober minded to consider the painting falling into malign hands?'

Linton did not answer.

'You will admit that the painting is not a true likeness?'

'It is an artist's likeness.'

'You altered facial features, lines of the body, yet wish this painting to be accepted as portraying Mrs Cane?'

'Yes.'

'To anyone but an artist, concerned with appearance rather than character, that seems an extravagant claim.'

'I don't accept that.'

'I suggest that the alterations to which you do admit were not made for any artistic reason but in order to persuade Mr Allun that Mrs Cane was in the dressing-room, not Miss Fowler.'

'On the abdomen, below the right breast, is a scar. If she was not Mrs Cane I was painting, why should I add a scar? How could I place it exactly in the correct position?'

'Have I not already made your possible reason clear?'

The cross-examination continued. Counsel were two verbal fencers, their foils words which constantly clashed but failed to gain the necessary three or five hits.

Quinn began his re-examination in the middle of the afternoon. 'Mr Linton, you have clearly defined the difference in your mind between the artistic and the sexual view of a nude female woman. Would you think many understand such distinction?'

'Any true artist would.'

'My learned friend suggests that in order to substantiate Mrs Cane's alibi, even though supported by your evidence, you believed it necessary to prove the lady in your studio on the twelfth was Mrs Cane, not Miss Fowler, and that to do this, you painted in a scar. Did you know Mrs Cane bore such a scar before you saw her naked?'

'No.'

'When did you first see her naked?'

'On the morning she came to the studio after she had run from home because her husband had assaulted her.'

'Until then, you had no reason to believe she bore such a scar?'

'No.'

'She had never casually mentioned it or referred to the accident?

'No.'

'So when you were painting this picture, you could not have accurately depicted the scar had you and Mrs Cane not recently made love?'

'No.'

'And by your evidence, that was on the twelfth of October.'

'Yes.'

'And this would not have happened had not Mrs Cane been driven from her house. Then clearly she could have had no part in her husband's death.'

'I tried again and again to make people understand that. I kept saying . . . But they wouldn't listen, and I couldn't succeed.'

'Thank you, Mr Linton.'

Linton left the court, convinced the alibi would be accepted, certain it would not. He drove to Springside Road, parked behind a car, began to walk towards No 36.

'Mr Linton.'

He came to a stop. The driver of the car spoke through a lowered window. His face seemed vaguely familiar, but Linton could not identify him. 'Yes?'

'Roger Groves, reporter with the *Harmsworth Gazette*. I'd be grateful for a word.'

'If it's about the case, forget it.'

'It won't take longer than a wagtail's wag.' Groves hurriedly climbed out of the car. 'I might be able to do you some good.'

'A magician?'

'A bit of publicity could do you wonders.'

Linton accepted it would be stupid to antagonize Groves. 'It's getting cold. Come in and have a drink.' He unlocked the front door, stepped to one side. 'Up the stairs and turn left.'

There was no gin or whisky left, only three cans of lager. He picked up two cans, two glasses, carried them through to the small, poorly furnished sitting-room, handed a can and glass to Groves, sat.

Groves opened his can, emptied it into the glass, raised this. 'Cheers.'

Linton did not respond.

'Is the painting here, Mr Linton?'

'At the studio.'

'Have you got a photo of it?'

'No.'

'How about driving to the studio and showing me?'

'Why?'

'So I can describe it accurately.'

'A reporter who talks about accuracy?'

Groves laughed. 'We're not quite as rare as hen's teeth.'

Linton drank.

'With your troubles, Mr Linton, I was surprised you didn't tell me to eff off.'

'Manners made me forgo the pleasure.'

'I thought it wouldn't do me any harm to write about your painting. Might make my editor appreciate my initiative.'

'A moment ago, your object was to do me some good.'

'A bit of a quid pro quo.'

There was humour in Groves' brashness. It temporarily shifted midnight thoughts from Linton's mind. 'Who gets the quid?'

They drove, in their respective cars, to the studio. Once inside, Groves remarked: 'Seems cold enough to freeze mine as well as the pawnbroker's. How d'you work in minus zero?'

'A bottled-gas fire and thermal woollens. The painting is over there.'

Groves walked over to the easel. 'But this is a clothed portrait.'

'A knowledgeable man!'

'I reckoned you were going to show me the painting they talked about in court.'

'Off limits.'

'Hope you don't mind me saying this is real good.'

'I never object to an unsolicited judgement which is favourable.'

'I could write about it in my article.'

'On limits.'

'It makes her look like she could never do in her husband.'

'Because she couldn't.'

'You think she'll get off then?'

'Depends what justice signifies.'

'How d'you mean?'

'Not certain.'

'How about a description of the other painting?'

'An appreciation of the female body.'

'Seemed a bit more than that when they talked about it in court.'

'Prudish people often have erotic imaginations.'

TWENTY-TWO

The summing-up was under way.

'. . . You will consider the question of motive. Did the accused have motive for wishing for her husband's death? You have heard that Mr Cane's business suffered a grave misfortune, which must by necessity have had severe results for his financial situation, to the extent he would very probably have had to sell his house, a distressing prospect for him and his wife. He possessed a life assurance, for a considerable sum, yet this could offer no relief from his problems while he lived; though, were he to die, his wife would not suffer such hardships as were he to continue to live . . .'

'Members of the jury, it will be obvious to you that should you accept the evidence of Mr Linton, Mrs Cane could not have been in her house at the time of her husband's death. Mr Allun delivered a pizza to Mr Linton on the day and within the period of time in which Mr Cane died. In the witness box, Mr Allun showed no uncertainty about identifying the painting on which Mr Linton had been engaged and that it was the one of which he was shown a photograph. Whilst in the studio, he heard a woman call out from the changing room, asking Mr Linton if he had seen her snakes. She modified this to explain she meant her brooch. Was that lady Mrs Cane or Miss Fowler? Since Mr Allun could only judge by the voice, it was arranged for him to hear both ladies speak. He was unable to identify with absolute certainty which of the two had spoken those words when dressing.

'You must ask yourselves: is there evidence to suggest which of the two ladies it was who, when in the dressing room, spoke?

Miss Fowler said she hated snakes to the extent she would never have worn a snake brooch. Why should she lie about this? Perhaps you will ask yourselves whether she enjoys a relationship with Mr Linton and wished to support him. There is no evidence of this. She has denied on oath it was she in the changing room that day.

'Mrs Cane says she likes snakes because, in the language of jewellery, it denotes the circle of love there is between two people, and the brooch was given to her by Mr Cane before their marriage. When the police asked to be shown the brooch, they were. She says she was in the dressing room in the studio after Mr Linton had finished working on her portrait. The prosecution claims it was Miss Fowler who was there. Yet when Mr Allun delivered the pizza, he saw the work he believed Mr Linton engaged on and you have heard the claim the subject was Mrs Cane . . .'

'Members of the jury, your task is to reach a verdict based solely on what you have heard in this court. You will dismiss from your minds any comments, any presumptions made outside the court-room; you will dismiss any judgement based solely on Mr Linton's artistic values and behaviour.

'You have a difficult task before you, but that must not deter you from your duty, which is to reach a verdict without fear or favour, based solely on what you have learned in court.'

Linton watched the jury leave the courtroom. Twelve men and women on whom depended Elaine's freedom and happiness. How strait-laced were the five women? Could they accept Elaine, married, would indulge in what might seem to them to be an orgy of sex, then allow herself to be painted in the nude in a risqué pose? Would the men, forgetting what she had suffered, not conscious of their jealous dislike because of the sexual passion she had enjoyed, find fault in her defence?

He found further reason for fear. The long wait for judgement meant there was no clear agreement. Were most of the jury voting guilty, and would the pressure of the large majority turn the verdict of the few . . .? His fear became panic when the court was informed that no unanimous verdict was likely to be reached quickly, so the jury would be taken to a hotel for the night and they would reassemble the next morning.

On the drive to his flat, he stopped at a Tesco supermarket and bought a bottle of gin and three bottles of tonic.

The court sat, except for the judge, who would be called when a verdict was reached. Counsel chatted, had token wagers on the verdict. The clerk of the court whistled through his teeth with monotonous regularity as he wondered what his wife would cook for supper.

After two and a quarter hours, judge and jury returned to court. The foreman was asked if a unanimous verdict had been reached? It had not. Were ten members of the jury of the same opinion? They were. Then a verdict could be accepted.

'Not guilty.'

In the CID general room the next day, Clements asked: 'Have you been on skag, Trist?'

'Why ask that?'

'What else could scramble your brains so hard that you can still think she didn't help him over the banisters?'

Hopkins entered. 'Trist, prepare papers for the CPS detailing Mr Linton's and Mrs Crane's perjury.'

'Are you serious, sarge?'

'You think I'm bloody joking, after twelve deaf and dumb freaks throw weeks of our work into the dustbin?'

'You don't accept the verdict?'

'A farce.'

'Sarge?' Lewis asked.

'What?'

'Do you think they'll be found guilty of perjury?'

'I don't think they'll be married in Canterbury Cathedral.'

'They had to lie in order to make certain she wouldn't be unjustly imprisoned. How can it be a criminal act to ensure justice is done?'

'Recruiting should have demanded you took a test for psychiatric disorder before accepting you into the force.'

Days after the end of the trial, black-bellied clouds forecast imminent rain and the north-easterly wind had cold fingers.

'How about going into town?' Lewis suggested.

'It's not very nice out, you said there was something you wanted to watch on telly and I suppose I ought to offer to help mother prepare lunch,' Audrey answered.

'I'm not fussed about the programme and thought it would be an idea to have a quick mooch around.'

'Then we'll go to M and S and see if they've a jacket that'll fit you.'

'I've already got one!'

'Which can't be thrown away soon enough.'

'You want to turn me into a tailor's dummy?'

She laughed. 'Even Savile Row couldn't manage to do that.'

Mrs Rayner came into the sitting room. 'I've run out of soft brown sugar and I need it for the cakes. D'you think you two could get some for me?'

'Why not use ordinary brown sugar?' Audrey suggested.

'That chef on the telly with the funny nose said it had to be soft brown sugar if the cake was to be really tasty. Bullens in Titchworth Road will have it.'

'We'll go right away,' Lewis said as he stood.

As they drove away from the semi-detached house with a front garden which confirmed Mrs Rayner's love of gardening – there was still colour in it – Audrey said: 'Are you trying to creep into my mother's good books?'

'I've been there since she first met me.'

'What amazing modesty!'

He took his hand off the steering wheel and patted her knee. 'No reason to be modest when I'm next to an entrancingly beautiful woman.'

'What's got into you, talking like that?'

'You object to deserved praise?'

'You're acting very oddly, talking about going out and rushing to help mother, when earlier you said you had to see that programme, and now talking like a two-bit gigolo.'

They drove past Titchworth Road.

'Where are you going, for heaven's sake?'

'Oh dear! What can I have been thinking of?'

'You'd better not tell me.'

'Since I've made a boo-boo, we might as well have a look at the shops.'

'We came out to get sugar.'

'We'll get it on the way back.'

'Back from where?'

'The foothills of Valhalla.'

'Have you been drinking? I'm worried. Please drive me home.'

He turned into High Street, found a vacant parking meter.

'You've got to tell me what's going on,' she said, her worry now great.

'There's something I want to show you.' He got out of the car, put a coin in the meter, opened the door for her. Worried, she hesitated before she stepped out.

He walked thirty yards, stopped in front of a jeweller's, opened the door for her.

'Morning, Mr Lewis,' Halliton, behind the counter, said. He used a key to open the back of the showcase counter, brought out a tray of diamond rings, put this down on the glass top.

She stared at the rings, then at Lewis.

'If you don't like any of them, Mr Halliton will show you some more,' he said.

He wandered away, not wanting to have any influence on her choice. He stared at the contents of a glass-fronted display cabinet against a side wall. She came across to where he stood, spoke in a low voice. 'Do you know what they cost?'

'I've a general idea.'

'But . . . they are so terribly expensive.'

'You don't like any of them?'

'Of course I do, but . . .'

'Choose one.'

'But . . .'

'But me no more buts. I promise you don't have to worry.'

He idly studied the display cabinet, his thoughts in the past. Until recently, he had been saving to buy her an engagement ring where value must lie in the emotion with which it would be given. Then he had received a solicitor's letter telling him an almost-forgotten uncle had left him many thousands of pounds. After he'd paid for the ring, there would still be enough money to provide the down payment on a mortgage . . . A brooch on the second shelf in the cabinet abruptly scrambled his thoughts.

'Darling, come here,' she called out.

He went over to where she stood.

'This is so lovely!' She held up her left hand to show him the solitaire diamond ring on her finger.

'Then leave it on.'

The soft brown sugar was forgotten on their drive home. She showed the ring to her mother, who was as emotional as she was; her father, more practical, opened a bottle of champagne.

Later, Lewis drove back to the jeweller's.

Halliton smiled. 'Your fiancée has decided she would like the ring a fraction wider?'

'I doubt she'll let it off her finger for a while, even if it is a bit tight. I'm back because I noticed a brooch in the show cabinet and wondered if you knew its history.'

'Which brooch is that?'

Lewis pointed to it. Halliton returned to the counter for a key, unlocked and opened the cabinet door, picked up the brooch. 'I was told it was from a place called Snake City, somewhere in India, where the snake is said to possess the soul of the dead. No marks, but silver of a low grade. I bought two examples many years ago, but sadly they did not attract attention. Follow custom and style, never try to jump ahead of them, as my father advised me to do many years ago. I find charm in native work, but it seems very few do. Judging by the description in the local newspaper, it could be a cousin of the one in the trial of Mrs Cane.'

'It does look as if it might be. You say you had two. What happened to the other?'

'Sold it recently, much to my surprise. A man brought a watch which needed a new battery, wandered around as I installed that, saw the two brooches and was so eager to have one, I half wondered if he knew something I didn't. Do you like it?'

'In a curious kind of way.'

'I now can only see it as an example of my youthful incompetence, so I'd be glad to be relieved of the reference. Is it sufficiently curious for you to be interested in a pleasant price?'

'How pleasant?'

'Thirty pounds.'

'I'll have it.'

Lewis left, walked along High Street. The memento from Snake City might have been well replicated for sale to tourists. Could there be any significance in the brooch's having been bought recently in the town Linton would probably use as his main shopping area? Mere circumstantial evidence?

He turned off High Street, came level with a small, enclosed public garden which commemorated the fallen in World War One. He went through the open gateway, along a path, sat. He stared at, without noting anything about it, a circular flower-bed which had been planted with bulbs. The woman dressing in Linton's studio had called out something along the lines of: 'Mike, have you seen my snakes . . .? My brooch, you idiot.' Betty Fowler had sworn she disliked snakes. In order to try to save the woman he loved, had Linton persuaded her to claim such dislike, since then it must seem it had not been she who had been dressing when Ted had delivered the pizza? Yet if Mrs Cane was to be believed to be the woman in the studio, she had to be ready to produce a snake brooch . . .

A verdict of Not Guilty no longer precluded a second trial for the same offence. Additional evidence could be produced. Then it would be determined whether Linton had been the buyer of the brooch that was companion to the one now in his coat pocket. Betty would be repeatedly questioned; the evidence must surely be uncovered that she had owned and worn a piece of jewellery with a snake motif. Ted might be blown by the wind of public opinion and finally decide he could identify who had called out in the studio.

His belief in justice demanded he explain his suspicions to Hopkins. Yet although he still believed Elaine was innocent, the proof she had lied about the brooch might ensure a guilty verdict. His unshaken conviction she could not have had any part in her husband's death legally couldn't carry the weight of a spider's web . . .

Mr and Mrs Rayner had gone out for the evening. Audrey and Lewis were eating at home. The beef stew had been very tasty, the dumplings light and not lumpy, the potatoes and runner beans beyond reproach, yet he had not offered one word of praise for her cooking. She reached across the table to pick up his empty plate. 'I'm sorry you didn't like it,' she said reprovingly. 'I tried to make you a really delicious meal, but you've hardly spoken, and you might as well have been eating scrag-end.'

'It was delicious.'

'There's no need to say that to try to please me.'

'I mean it, a hundred times over . . . I'm sorry, but I'm worried to hell and don't know what to do.'

Her annoyance became irrational fear. 'You . . . you've changed your mind?'

'About what?'

'Us?'

'How d'you mean?'

'Maybe . . . maybe you think you've made a mistake.'

'You can't think . . . Darling, the wedding can't come quickly enough. It's work that's getting me down.'

She put her plate back on the table, walked round, stood behind his chair and put her arms around him. 'Can't you leave all that back at the station?'

'That won't stop the questions. It'll only make them louder.'

'What questions?'

'Like: should one do the right thing for the wrong reason, or the wrong thing for the right reason? If justice is truth, how can it be found with lies?'

She leaned over to rest her cheek against his. 'I can't understand what you're on about, my love, but I know you'll always do what you believe to be right.'